GORDON D. SHIRREFFS

HANGIN' PARDS

Complete and Unabridged

LINFORD
Leicester

First Linford Edition
published August 1988

British Library CIP Data

Shirreffs, Gordon D.
   Hangin' pards.—Large print ed.—
Linford western library
I. Title
813'.54[F]

ISBN 0-7089-6531-8

Published by
F. A. Thorpe (Publishing) Ltd.
Anstey, Leicestershire
Set by Rowland Phototypesetting Ltd.
Bury St. Edmunds, Suffolk
Printed and bound in Great Britain by
T. J. Press (Padstow) Ltd., Padstow, Cornwall

1

HOLT DEAVER squinted his eyes against the glare of the desert sun and looked to the east toward the base of the shimmering Kofas. The whole land seemed ablaze beneath the torrent of heat and light poured down from above. The mountains seemed to lift and waver in the moving air. There was a spiraling thread of saffron dust rising from the desert floor about three or four miles from where Holt Deaver sat his tired sorrel. He slid from his saddle and squatted in the scant shade of the horse, eyeing the mushrooming dust while he felt for the makings and began to roll a smoke.

"Nobody but a damned fool would ride a horse at that speed beneath this sun," said Holt as he lighted up.

He glanced back over his shoulder. The yellow flood of the Colorado was miles behind him now. They had recrossed it

1

in the dark of the moon downriver from Old Ehrenburg and had kept on across the desert all that night and morning. Now it was high noon and the sorrel was in trouble. For that matter so was Holt, for his water had run out and he knew well enough if Alamo Springs was dry he'd probably lose the sorrel and maybe himself. It was a long way to the Gila on foot from Alamo Springs.

Holt sucked in on his cigarette as he teetered on his feet. The heat of the sand and decomposed stone soaked up through his thin boot soles. It was then that he noticed that there was another, thicker rising column of dust several miles behind the first one he had seen. That wasn't unusual in the desert, for he had often seen several wind-devils spiraling upward in the hot air at the same time.

But he saw something glinting at the base of the second dust column, and he saw dark dots moving. Men riding fast and following right on the trail of whatever was causing the first column of dust. Yuma Pen was about fifty miles or so downriver and this desert had seen more than one escaped convict get run down before he could reach the mountains. The Mohaves and the Yumas made quite a business out of tracking down fugitives from the Arizona hellhole. Many times they didn't bother to bring the man in alive; just his head in a gunny sack. The payment was the same and it saved a lot of trouble. The prison officials didn't care either. One less half-mad inmate to deal with. The place was overcrowded anyway.

Holt rubbed his bristly chin. He was damned glad it wasn't him who was running from Yuma. He was *running*, sure enough, but not from bloodthirsty and merciless Indian trackers. Somewhere behind him was Trump Foster and Morgan Mills who had been following him since he had been involved in a bit of hot gunplay in a grove of cottonwoods not far from Fort Mohave. Holt had been camped there at about the same time Foster and Mills had shown up. He knew them well enough. Both of them had been evading a stretch in Yuma Pen and the hangman for a good many years. With them had been Mike Mills, younger brother of Morgan, as wild an owlhoot as Holt had ever met.

Foster and the Mills boys had divulged a plan to Holt. Appropriations for army pay had been late, so the paymaster was carrying several months pay. The outlaws wanted to hit him for the money and had asked Holt, not too politely, to throw in with them. He had refused and had pulled out, only to go back for something he had left behind. Just in time to see the robbery and cold-blooded killing of the paymaster and his small escort. Holt had pulled out again; he had wanted no part of the outlaws or anything to do with robbing the government. But Mike Mills had tried to stop him, and when the gun smoke had cleared the kid was dead and Holt was on the run.

The dust was moving toward Alamo Springs. Holt had to get there first. He needed that water, and if there was any left they'd be welcome to it.

Holt had the edge on distance, but maybe they could travel faster. He spurred the sorrel despite his pity for the weary horse. It was either that, or death in the desert. He looked back toward the Colorado. There was a faint skein of yellow dust rising there too and he wasn't about to sit around on his hunkers waiting to see who *that* was. He had a pretty good idea who was making that dust.

He was concealed by a long, low ridge that rose from the baking desert floor, but he could still see the movement to the east as he drove the sorrel on and on. When he was at last climbing the lower flanks of the Kofas he knew the horse would never make it. They reached the highest point of the shallow pass and Holt slid from the saddle. The sorrel stood straddle-legged, head low, caked with dried lather.

A furnace wind swept steadily around man and horse as they stood there. Then Holt took his rifle and canteen, pulled down the brim of his dusty hat to shade his eyes against the glare of the sun and slogged down toward the springs. He did not look back, for he didn't have the heart to do so.

He made good time on foot and then as he rounded a knoll he saw the springs. After plunging down the slope he saw that there was hardly enough water for one man, let alone those others who were coming toward the springs. He drank sparingly, then filled his canteen, then drank again. There was just about enough water to get him to the Gila, but he'd suffer on the way.

There were horses being ridden by the strangers who were heading for the springs. A hard glint shone in Holt Deaver's eyes. He left the springs and walked slowly up a slope until he could look to the south, and then he saw a lone figure struggling up the incline. A mile and a half more behind the lone man he could see four horsemen walking their horses. Maybe they were sure of their game now. "I wonder why he's running?" he said to himself. He lifted his Winchester and levered a round into the chamber, then slid into a hollow that had the heat of a baker's oven in it. There he could watch to see what happened, and if he was lucky, he could snatch a horse. He had never stolen a horse in his life, but this was no time to be choosy. He had to make Sonora within the next few days and he knew well enough he couldn't make it alone.

The man on foot was making heavy weather of it. Now and then raising an arm to wipe his face he would look back, then flog himself on with a peculiar running, hopping gait until he slowed down again to a stumbling, wavering walk. The hot wind played fitfully with his ragged, grayish-white beard. He was no spring chicken but he had plenty of steam in him for his age. The heat and exertion would have felled many a younger man than him.

Holt touched his dry lips with the tip of his tongue. There was a mouthful or two of water in the spring, no more. Just enough to tease the old-timer when he got there. Certainly there wasn't enough to carry him on to the north to the Wickenburg-Ehrenburg Road; not in that blazing heat at any rate. To the west was the river and plenty of water. To the east was nothing but baking mountains and desert—and death.

There should have been more pity in Holt Deaver than he now felt. But an outlaw had to take care of himself first or he'd lose the bloody game and there'd be no second chance, not for Holt Deaver at least. He had been moving south after a gambling and shooting scrape in Chloride, and for all he knew a posse might be on his trail too. He wasn't too worried about them. He had outridden posses before, but with Trump Foster and Morg Hills it would be another matter. Not only for the killing of Mike Mills, but also for his witnessing the payroll robbery would they want to wipe him out. They'd never let up until they did.

So Holt Deaver had to have a horse. He had his water, and there were four horses being ridden slowly toward the springs. One of those horses was going to be ridden *from* those springs by Holt Deaver.

The strange chase that was being run before his eyes began to intrigue him. The old man wasn't going to win it, of course, and Holt almost felt a twinge of pity for him; but it was a fleeting thought. But you had to give the old man a grudging thought of respect for putting up such a helluva struggle.

Then he saw one of the horsemen leisurely raise a rifle and then fire it. The slug screamed from the hard earth a few feet from the old man. The rifle flatted off two more times, raising faint spurts of dust from the ground, whipping the old man on and on so that now he was running in a shambling sort of way.

Holt wiped the sweat from his face. There was no need for them to crucify the old man. They had him cold. He could see the man's face plainly now as he tended a little toward Holt's hideout. The horsemen plodded on and the rifleman raised his rifle once more. It cracked and the old man spun about and fell heavily. His left foot had been shorn of its heel. Tophole shooting, if it had been intended to do what it did.

The old man bellied along the furnace-top ground and Holt could see every one of his agonized features. Bullet after bullet ripped into the ground near him. *Blast them! Why didn't they let him alone?*

Then the old man saw Holt. "For God's sake!" he gasped. "I don't know who you are, but if you hold off them buzzards I'll make you a rich man!"

"Sure, sure," said Holt softly.

"I ain't lyin'! I'll give you five thousand dollars in bills if you hold them back! Word of honor."

Holt grinned. "Yep," he said. "Word of honor. You old coot! Your tack is drove. Five thousand? What the hell! Make it ten thousand!"

The old man nodded. "All right! But hold 'em off!"

The horsemen had drawn rein now and were looking toward the old man. Holt wondered if they had seen him.

"If you're worried about them being lawmen you can forget it," said the fugitive.

Holt glanced quickly at him and an impatient feeling sped through him. He rubbed his bristly jaws. He needed a horse and he was going to get one.

One of the men fired and the shot screamed thinly from the rock near Holt driving tiny shards against his face. "Gawd dammit!" he snarled. They had seen him now and they were shooting to kill.

He rested the Winchester on the rock, took up the trigger slack, and fired an instant before one of the men did. His slug had whipped through the closest man's hat. He bent low and spurred off. Holt fired again, creasing the horse. It buck-jumped, threw the man heavily, and galloped toward Holt and the old man. Maybe he had smelled the water.

The old man rolled into the hollow and grinned evilly. "Good stuff, *amigo*! Keep shootin'! But aim to kill! Give me that gun! I'll show you!"

Holt turned fiercely. "Shut up!" he snapped.

He fired again and this time one of the men slid from his horse and darted into a hollow. The two other men were dashing madly to the south toward a sheltering ridge. Holt sent a slug whispering over their heads to spur them on.

The horse trotted past Holt and the old man, heading for the springs. Holt spoke out of the side of his mouth. "Go get him! Keep him away from the springs until you get a drink. One more thing." Holt turned. "Don't you take off on that horse, hombre. He's *mine. Comprende?*"

"*Yo comprendo!*"

The old man crawled from the hollow, reached up for the reins of the dun, then grinned at Holt. "You just made yourself ten thousand dollars." Then he was gone.

Holt refilled his rifle magazine and squatted low, wishing for a smoke. The two riders had vanished. The downed man still lay where he had fallen. The man in the hollow was not to be seen, but his horse was trotting back to where the other men had gone.

"Hot as sin," said Holt. He glanced at his canteen, wondering if the loco old coot had found water. There might be a mouthful or two still in the rock water pan.

When he heard a whispering sound coming from the slope, Holt glanced down. The man lay there, grinning like a gargoyle. "Water seepin' in," he said hoarsely. "I dug out a rock or two with my hands. Water seepin' in!"

Holt nodded.

"We can pull out as soon as I water that horse."

"We ain't going anywhere," said Holt dryly. "Leastways, not right now. Those hombres are still waiting out there. Who are they?"

"Sidewinders! They're following me for my money."

"You carrying money in those rags?"

Old Whiskers chuckled. He tapped the side of his head. "No. But it's up here."

Empty of brains. Full of money, thought Holt.

Holt crouched down and lit a cigarette. He never took his eyes from that man in the hollow. The fourth man still lay motionless on the baking ground. It was then that Holt noticed the awkward angle of the man's neck. His neck had been broken. A cold feeling came over him despite the furnace heat. Holt Deaver *killed* again.

Holt sucked in on his cigarette, then raised his rifle and fired across the hollow where the man lay hidden. The man leaped out of it and raced down the slope trailing his rifle. It was an old dodge to fire across a hollow like that, for the slug would crack over a man's head like a mule skinner's lash, and no matter how safe he was from getting hit, the sound of the slug was enough to put a chill into him.

"There'll be a moon tonight, Old Whiskers," said Holt over his shoulder. "I'll hold them off until dark, then I'll skin out. And I ain't riding double. You'll be on your own."

"Which way you going?"

"South."

"The money is north."

"Yeh. The North Pole maybe?"

"You made a verbal deal with me, didn'tcha?"

Holt looked at him. The old coot was far gone. "Who are you anyway?" he asked curiously.

"Cass Riker."

Holt stared at him, then grinned. "You lyin' old goat! Cass Riker has been dead for years."

"Nope. I'm Cass Riker all right."

Holt studied him. He had seen an old Wanted poster in a post office in Tucson some years ago, kept there as a curiosity, and that had been years after Cass Riker had been placed in hot storage at Yuma Pen after his big haul from the Southern Overland Mail. There was a vague resemblance between the hard-bitten face Holt had seen on the poster and the raddled, lined and bewhiskered countenance of the old man.

The old man grinned. "You know the

story. Cass Riker got away with the biggest haul in years and went to the pen before he'd confess where it was."

Holt nodded.

"They never did find it," said the old man. "And they never will."

"How so?"

The grin wrinkled up the old face. "Because I'm the only man who knows where it is, that's why!"

"Up north?"

"Up north."

"I'm heading south."

"Go on south," jeered the old man. "Go on! You won't make it! Sure, you *might* get to the border, but you won't get past the Rurales in Sonora lessn' you pay them off. What're you going to do in Mexico anyways? Punch cows for some ranchero? Come on, boy, help Old Cass Riker get north and I'll pay off what I owe you."

Holt touched his lips with the point of his tongue. The old man was loco, but maybe so was he.

"Say, Old Whiskers," Holt began

inquisitively. "How much was in that haul you made from the Southern Overland anyways?"

"Eighty thousand, bub. Eighty thousand."

Holt glanced quickly toward the old man, but Riker had vanished like a gecko lizard. Eighty thousand! A man could live like a king in Mexico with that kind of *dinero*. The best of everything! Horses, food and likker, and *women*. Holt thoughtfully fired another shot toward the south. He had some thinking to do before it grew dark.

2

IT was intensely dark before the rising
of the desert moon. Holt squatted
beside a pinnacle of rock with his
Winchester across his thighs. Riker had
dug out the springs, and they had had
their fill of the gamy water.

No chances were taken with the old
buzzard. The dun was picketed within
fifty feet of Holt. Riker was poking about
somewhere in the thick blackness out
there. The man was like a cat in the darkness. His past had slowly come back to
Holt. He had been a kid when the old
man had made his big strike over the
barrel of a shotgun in the gunpowder
blasted innards of a way station in the
Dragoons. That had been in 1870, fifteen
years ago, and when Riker had been
captured he had been sentenced to Yuma.
Both of his *compadres* in the holdup had
mysteriously disappeared between the

18

time of the holdup and the capturing of Cass Riker. They had never been found again.

A cold feeling came over Holt as he squatted there in the velvet obscurity. Supposing the old lizard did have it cached away? It might be worth a gamble to go north with Riker. But they'd have to move fast with Riker being followed by that trio, and the two outlaws from up north on his trail. Sonora seemed farther and farther away.

Riker came up the slope. "Got me a rifle," he said.

"Where'd you get it?"

"That dead *hombre* out there didn't need it no longer."

"You might of got a slug through your thick head!"

"You worried?"

"Not about you! I'm worried about that ten thousand bucks that doesn't exist!"

Riker spat. "You'll get it! But you got to help me get up north."

Holt tilted his head to one side. "Yeh," he said softly, "and when we do get up north I might get paid off in lead instead of gold. I oughta take that rifle and that beat-up old sixgun away from you."

"You ain't goin' to take *anything* from me, bub," said Riker softly, as he aimed the Winchester at Holt's belly. "You see?" Riker said. "I can kill you easy. I can take that hoss and the water and dust up a storm getting out of here and I wouldn't have to pay my debt to you."

Holt breaking out in a cold sweat, could see the set, dim face of the old man. He was right, there wasn't any doubt about that. Him and his blasted ten thousand eagles!

Then Riker lowered the rifle and let down the hammer to half cock. "But I give my word," he said simply.

Holt felt his pulse slow down. "Yeh . . . *gracias*," he said uneasily.

Something moved in the darkness beyond them. Holt gripped Riker by a shoulder and forced him down while he peered through the darkness with cocked Winchester at hip level, aimed right at the moving patch of shadow.

He was just about to fire when he heard a faint whinny. He stared. "Jesus," he said unbelievingly. "It's my horse."

Holt walked to the sorrel and passed an arm about its neck. "Leastways he don't smell as bad as you do, old man," he said over his shoulder. "Stay here and keep watch while I water him."

He led the sorrel down to the springs and watered him. The horse seemed to be all right now, but he was still pretty well worn out.

There was a faint suggestion of moonlight in the eastern sky. Time to get moving. Holt didn't want to go north, but he couldn't go south now, not with those three men waiting out there. Besides, Foster and Mills would have been making time while Holt had been trapped at the springs. He'd have to go north, for a time at least.

He walked up the slope. Then he stiffened as he heard the voice carry to the springs on the wind. "Hey you, Cass Riker!"

Cass did not move.

"We know you're there, Riker! You and that killer you got with you! We don't know how you arranged meeting him here. Pretty slick, Riker!"

The old man spat in the direction of the voice.

"Look, Riker! We're in a bad way for water! You let us get to those springs and we'll turn back south in the morning!"

"Sure, sure," said Cass *sotto voce*. "You'll turn back allright. In a pigs' butt you will!"

Holt peered through the darkness. He was beginning to distinguish things a little better now, and he realized that in a little while the desert would be silvered with clear light.

"Come on!" he said fiercely to the old man.

"Wait!"

Holt shook a fist at Riker.

"Riker! Let us get some water!"

"OK, Carley! Come on in, in about ten minutes."

Cass slid down the slope toward the springs.

Holt peered into the darkness again. Carley . . . the name teased his mind. It sounded vaguely familiar.

Riker was fooling around down by the springs. Then he looked at Holt. "You ready?"

"Yes."

"Let's pull out then."

They led the two horses to the north, tending a little easterly, toward the Harquahala Plains. Beyond the plains were more mountains. Holt looked back toward the springs. The wind had shifted, bringing the sound of grating footsteps to the two fleeing men.

Riker turned and fired a shot toward the springs. There was a muffled curse echoing the sound of the shot. "Ten minutes!" the old man yelled.

They moved out faster then, striding through the darkness, with their boot soles husking against the harsh earth. It would be a hell of heat again as soon as the sun came up, and by noon they must have water again. There were other springs and waterholes out there in the darkness, but Holt wasn't quite sure where they were. It had been a long time ago he had been through that country. He had been in the army then as government scout. There were times when he wished he had stayed in that service.

"You know your way to the water-holes?" asked Riker.

"Yes."

"You don't sound very sure of yourself, bub."

"You want to try it alone?" demanded Holt.

Riker did not answer. He knew well enough he had to depend on this rawboned companion of his, for a time at least. Until they found water again, and he was sure of his way. After that, well ten thousand was a helluva lot of dinero to pay for a guide.

"Carley," said Holt at last. "Who is he?"

"Ernie Carley. Think hard, *amigo*."

Holt stared at the old man. "He was one of the two *compadres* you had with you in that holdup!"

Riker cackled. "You recollect the other one?"

"Savvy Harris, wasn't it? Savvy Harris the gunslinger?"

"Keno," said Cass. "He's back there too. The third man is Pete Shalen. You remember who he was?"

Holt shoved back his hat. "There was a Pete Shalen who was a Wells-Fargo guard at the time of the holdup, wasn't there?"

"You're a lot brighter than I thought you was."

"Was he in on the deal too?"

"Keno."

"You played it pretty cosy, didn't you? That is, until they put you away in Yuma."

"You figure they outsmarted me then?"

"Fifteen years worth, old timer."

"Yeh, but tell me, bub, who knows where the *dinero* is? All eighty thousand of it?"

The new moon was tipping the eastern ranges and Holt could see the sly grin on the face of Cass Riker. "You're joshing me," said Holt.

Riker shook his head. "I paid fifteen years of hell for that money, bub, and I aim to keep it for myself. Less ten thousand of course. That's for you."

"Oh sure, I figgered it was."

"You still don't believe me?"

Holt strode on a few more paces. "I don't know what to believe," he said. He looked back over his shoulder. Ernie Carley and Savvy Harris! Those two sidewinders were sure death if you crossed them. And Pete Shalen had been known at the time of the robbery as one of the toughest Wells-Fargo agents in the business. "Who was the man I killed," he said at last.

"Oh, *him*? That was Webb Harris, Savvy's kid brother."

Holt looked back again. Now he had Trump Foster, Morg Mills, Ernie Carley, Savvy Harris and Pete Shalen dogging him, and all he had for comfort was a crazy old coot who claimed he owed Holt ten thousand dollars.

"Yup," said Cass. "I figgered it this way: Fifteen years against eighty thousand dollars works out at about five thousand, three hundred and thirty-three dollars a year. Course, I owe you ten thousand. I wisht you'd taken me up on the five thousand offer, but I was in no position to bargain, was I?"

"No," said Holt dryly. "You wasn't."

"Now, that leaves me seventy thousand. Let me figger." Riker looked up, half closed his eyes, wiggled his fingers and his whiskers, then glanced at Holt with gimlet eyes. "That gives me about four thousand, six hundred and sixty-six bucks per annum, don't it?"

Holt stared at Riker. The thought was almost incredible. To trade fifteen years of your life for that kind of money. It didn't make sense, and yet here was Cass Riker, who had certainly been the brains of the Wells-Fargo holdup, and who had never confessed that he knew where the loot was, telling Holt that that was exactly what he had done.

Holt glanced at the old man. He was

loco. But Holt hadn't seen any eighty thousand dollars, much less the ten thousand the old rummy said he owed Holt. Still, Holt couldn't get to Sonora for a time, nor could he head west for California. So he'd have to bear north until he could swing back south again. He was twenty-five years old, dead broke and on the run, and he had shot one man in Chloride and had killed two others in less than a week. Ten thousand bucks! It was worth more than a second thought, unless Cass Riker was playing Holt for the fool. There was always one way out; he could wring the truth out of the old coot if he had to.

The moon now flooded the desert, silvering the hard surface of it, etching shadows of rock and thorny growths against it in fantastic patterns. Holt looked back. "If they get enough water they won't waste any time tailing us," he said.

Riker cackled. "Sure, sure!" He cackled again.

Holt looked closely at the old man.

"What's so funny about that?" he demanded.

Riker explored his scraggly beard, scratching vigorously, and then he glanced back over his shoulder. "That water taste sort of gamy to you? Brackish like too?"

"Yes."

The old man grinned. "It'll taste a helluva lot more brackish when they get there. Course they won't really notice it, because they can't afford to be too fussy. Leastways, they won't notice anything for *awhile*."

"What do you mean?"

Riker yawned. "I dropped a handful of chloral hydrate into that rock pan. I figgered there was enough water to thin it out so's it wouldn't be noticed right away."

"Chloral hydrate? Knockout drops?"

"Yup."

"Why, you dirty old—"

Riker held up a hand. "Maybe you coulda thought of a better way to stop 'em? Hellsfire, all you can think of is shooting, and not too good at that."

"You figured I should have killed them?"

The hard eyes of the old man seemed to bore a hole into Holt's eyes. "Why not? They woulda killed *you*."

Holt felt for the makings. He was beginning to wonder what kind of a mad partnership he had made with this loony old man. Still, he had been on foot, and had needed a horse.

"For ten thousand bucks, I could do a lot of killing," said Cass Riker. "Give me them makings, *amigo*."

Holt looked back after he had lighted his cigarette. Chloral hydrate would stop them sure enough, *if* they had imbibed enough of the gamy water from the springs.

He'd have to watch the old man. He was slick as grease and as deadly as a diamondback. Holt had saved him back there at Alamo Springs, and was now helping him to escape. Riker could have gone on alone, of course, but Holt had a feeling that Riker didn't know the country. He needed Holt. For a time at least he wouldn't try any of his tricks on Holt.

"Just where are we heading, Riker?" he asked.

"Northeast, bub, to the next waterhole."

"You know where that is?"

Riker looked quickly at Holt. He drew in on his cigarette and the sudden flareup of light illuminated his face. "No, I don't, bub. But you do."

"Supposing I don't?"

There was a moment's silence, then Riker laughed. "You wouldn't be damned fool enough to come north with me 'less you *did* know where water was. Now, where is it?"

Holt grinned. "Well, Old Whiskers, seems like you *hired* me to find it, so I will, but I ain't telling you where it is until we get there."

"Supposing something happens to you before then? I'd die out here, bub."

"What can happen to me, Old Whiskers?"

The old man did not answer. He sucked in on the last of his cigarette and then dropped it, grinding it under a boot sole. "You mean you don't trust me, bub? Old Cass Riker?"

"Old *Honest* Cass Riker, you mean don't you?"

The old man stared at him a moment and then he laughed softly. "Keno," he said.

Beyond the desert, to the northeast, were mountains where a man could easily lose himself, or anyone following him. But Holt knew his way through the tangle. He had worked out of Whipple Barracks near Prescott, and also from Camp Verde in the days when the Apaches had been on the warpath. Holt wasn't worried about finding his way through those mountains, and once they were up there, they'd have no water problem. That would be Riker's chance to get rid of Holt.

In all probability, Riker's story of his

cache was as nebulous and legendary as the Dutchman's Lost Mine or the Lost Adams Diggings. Now Holt was stuck with the old man until he could make his own getaway to the south, the long way around. But the old coot was so sure of himself!

3

HOLT DEAVER lay flat on the ridge top looking down upon the little settlement. He had been there for over an hour, watching the movements of the people down there. He knew the place, for he had passed through often enough when he had been scouting. Yardigan it was called, after old Pop Yardigan, the man who had settled there right after the war, fighting off Apaches to make his place in the mountains. The man had done well enough too. His was the only general store and blacksmithing place for many a mile.

Holt rolled the last of his tobacco into a paper and lighted it. He and the old man needed food, tobacco and cartridges before they plunged further into the mountains. Cass had insisted that Holt go for the stores. The old man had an obsession that everyone in the territory

34

knew he was free from Yuma Pen at last and was on his way to his cache. Holt had been an honest man when he had last been in this area. Even if he was recognized he'd probably be able to carry it off.

The three men who trailed them, if they had recovered from the chloral hydrate in time, would certainly know Riker on sight, but none of them had seen Holt. They didn't worry him half as much as the two men who had been following him from the Colorado. Still, they had no way of knowing which way he had gone from Alamo Springs.

Holt sucked in on his smoke. His belly writhed in hunger. He had wanted to kill some game but Old Whiskers had been against shooting to let anyone know where they were. He was as cautious as an old woman that way.

Holt shrugged. He stood up, eased his Colt in its holster, then led the sorrel down the slope. He had taken Riker's saddle, for a man riding bareback would be a little suspicious-looking. Riker had given Holt ten dollars, profits from Riker's years in Yuma.

Holt tethered his horse to the hitching rail and looked up and down the single street. There was no one in sight. He stepped up onto the warped porch and looked into the store. The place was a jungle of merchandise, stacked against the walls, lining the aisles, hung from wires strung from wall to wall. He walked in and looked toward the rear of the store to where a man was standing behind a battered counter making entries in a thick ledger.

Holt glanced back out of the door once more. The place was on a trail that was used quite a bit. If Holt had been trailing anyone from the area from which he and the old man had come, he would have tried this trail first for results. He'd get his supplies as quickly as he could and then pull out of there.

Holt walked to the back of the store. It was Old Man Yardigan standing there. He glanced up as he saw Holt. "Howdy? He'p you?"

The young man now gave him his supply order.

"Right." The old man peered at Holt. "You look familiar."

It had been almost four years since Holt had been in that area. He had leaned out a good deal since then and in those days he had sported a short reddish beard.

"You working around here?" asked Yardigan.

"Passing through."

"North or south?"

"North. Say, can I have that stuff now?" Holt placed his penciled list on the counter.

"Sure, sure. You in a hurry?" asked Yardigan a little suspiciously.

"No, but I don't aim to spend the whole day here. Have to make miles before sundown."

"All right." Yardigan began to study the list as though it was some rare medieval hand-illuminated manuscript.

Holt wet his lips. He reached over the counter and snagged a bag of Pride of Durham. "Add this one," he said. He rolled a smoke and lighted it, drawing the smoke deeply into his lungs.

Yardigan moved slowly, placing the articles on the counter. He looked up at Holt. "I got everything here except the cartridges. Just happen to have run out of forty-fours. You know how popular that caliber is. Happens there is a shipment came in last night from Wickenburg and I ain't separated it yet."

"I need them."

"Look, it's going to take some time to get these cartridges. Whyn't you go across the street and have a beer or something?"

"I'm in a hurry, mister."

"Sure. Everyone is in a hurry these days. You want those cartridges or not?"

Holt nodded. He walked to the doorway. He could use a drink. He hadn't had one since Mormon Crossing.

Holt walked across the street to the saloon and pushed through the sagging batwings. The big room was empty except for a bald-headed barkeep reading a newspaper at the end of the long bar. The barkeep looked up. "Your pleasure?"

"Rye."

Bottle and glass slid to a stop in front of Holt. He poured a drink.

The bartender looked up. "Passing through?"

Holt nodded as he raised the glass to his lips.

"Keep an eye open for an old man with a beard. Crusty old coot. He just got sprung out of Yuma so this paper says. Name of Cass Riker."

Holt lowered the glass. How the devil had that gotten into a newspaper so fast? "Cass Riker? Who is he?" he asked quietly.

The bartender eyed him. "You must be a stranger all right. Everyone in this territory knows about Cass Riker. Made a big haul from Wells-Fargo fifteen years ago. Then he got picked up and spent fifteen years in the *juzgado* but they never did find the money. Over a hundred thousand it was they say."

Holt downed his drink. That was a clear profit of twenty thousand if it was true. He refilled his glass.

"Old Cass was too smart for 'em though. Never let on where that money was. They say he was offered a shorter sentence if he'd say where the money was. He never did though."

"So he's loose now?"

"I guess so. This paper doesn't say he was let loose. Just that he was about to be let loose." The bartender grinned. "I'll bet every hardcase in the territory will be keeping an eye out for him. A hundred thousand! A fortune, friend, a fortune. Cass Riker even double-crossed his partners on the deal. They'll be hot after him, too."

"I seem to remember some of the story now. Didn't the law think that Riker did away with Carley and Harris?"

"Hell, Riker went into the pen to get *away* from Carley and Harris."

"You're sure about that?"

The bartender came down to the end of the bar, took a glass and filled it, then leaned toward Holt. "I am," he said mysteriously. "And I can tell you something else I know." He looked behind

40

him as though a lawman was listening right at his back. "I seen Carley and Harris not more 'an two weeks ago."

"Where?"

"Right here, friend. They come in here with a couple of other *hombres* and drank right there!"

Holt downed his drink. "What do you think they're up to?"

The man grinned. "They wasn't going south for their health. They looked like they'd been in these mountains for some time. I had a feeling they was going down to wait for Cass Riker to get sprung."

Holt nodded. He could feel the liquor warming up his empty gut. There was a cold feeling within him. He was sure now that Riker was heading for his cache, with the bloodhounds hard on his heels, and he had Holt Deaver with him as an almost unwilling ally. But what had Carley and Harris been doing in the mountains? Maybe they had a rough idea of where Riker had hidden the loot.

The batwings swung open and a big, broad-shouldered man walked in. "Beer,"

41

he said to the bartender. He nodded to Holt and Holt had a cold feeling again. The man had lawman stamped across his broad face. Holt nodded.

"Hello, Stuart," said the bartender.

"Howdy, Baldy. Any news?"

"Cass Riker is out of Yuma."

Stuart nodded. "I knew that."

"You looking for him?"

"No. That's someone else's responsibility. I'm working on something else."

"So?"

Stuart sipped his beer and glanced casually at Holt. "Payroll robbery near Fort Mohave. Paymaster Rascobb and four troopers were shot down from ambush and the payroll was taken. They say four men were in on it. A grave was found in a grove of cottonwoods near the scene of the robbery."

"What was in it? The money?"

Stuart shook his head. "A man shot to death. No name and no identification. The other three were supposed to have headed south along the Colorado. We don't know if they crossed over to the

California side or whether they're heading for Sonora. My guess is Sonora."

Holt felt a cold sweat trickle down his sides. He wanted to get out of there in a hurry.

"They got any idea who did the job?"

"Not yet. They think a man by the name of Deaver was mixed up in it. He had been in a shooting scrape in Chloride and had been seen near Fort Mohave."

Holt refilled his glass and held it tightly to keep his hand from shaking.

A boy poked his tousled head beneath the batwing doors. "Say, mister," he said to Holt, "your things is ready at the store."

He flipped the kid a two-bit piece. "Thanks." He paid his tab and emptied his glass. "See you later," he said with a smile.

Without looking back, he crossed, stepped up onto the store porch and entered the store. He took his sack of supplies and paid for them.

Yardigan leaned back against the shelving behind him. He squinted at

Holt. "I'm sure I seen you somewheres, friend."

Holt smiled. "Not likely. First time I've been through here."

"So? You got a twin brother or something like that?"

"No."

"Hmmm . . . I never forget a face. I'll think of it after you're gone."

I hope to God you don't, thought Holt.

He walked to the door and peered out. His heart sank as he saw three horsemen riding slowly down the slope from the south. He recognized them at once— Ernie Carley, Savvy Harris and Pete Shalen.

Holt stepped back into the store. He walked to the rear. "Say," he said quickly. "There's a man over in the saloon. Name of Stuart. You know him?"

The storekeeper looked curiously at Holt. "Sure. That's Burl Stuart, Deppity United States Marshal for these parts."

"Thanks. I thought he was a lawman. He's looking for three men."

"I know. That Fort Mohave thing."

"Keno! Well, I just looked outside and saw three men riding toward here. Trail-dusty and tired-out looking."

"So?"

"Stuart said he was looking for three men who did the job near Fort Mohave. Get it?"

Yardigan's eyes widened. He reached for his cash box.

"No time for that!" said Holt crisply. "Get over to the saloon and tell Stuart."

"Why don't you go?"

Holt smiled mysteriously. "Because I'm working undercover on the same case. Now git!"

"Sure! Sure!"

Holt followed the storekeeper to the front door. Yardigan hurried across the street. Holt slung his sack of provisions across his saddle cantle and untethered the sorrel, keeping it between him and the three approaching riders. He was leading the sorrel around the side of the store when he heard one of the men yell, then he heard the beating hoofs on the hard ground.

He swung up on his horse and sank the steel into his flanks, racing across an open field for a rail fence at the rear of it. A gun flatted off but he did not look back. They took the fence easily.

Another gun cracked. Holt looked back and saw Burl Stuart standing on the porch of the saloon with a pistol in his hand. The three hardcases were fighting their plunging, rearing horses in the middle of the street.

The man and his horse shot past the pines and was thudding up on a ridge when he heard a faint yelling carried to him on the breeze. "I know who that *hombre* was!" cried Yardigan. "Useta be in the army! Name of Holt Deaver!"

Now Stuart would be after him, as well as Carley, Harris and Shalen, for the last three would know he had been the man with Riker back at Alamo Springs. Now all that had to happen to make things real sporting would be to have Morg Mills and Trump Foster show up.

He circled widely, dismounting to lead the tired sorrel up a steep slope, then down into a ravine which he followed until he reached the road far south of Yardigan. He crossed the road in a hurry, and vanished into the woods. The camp was three miles west of town.

Carley, Harris and Shalen would have a helluva time explaining things to Burl Stuart, but Yardigan had given Holt away, and Stuart would have a hot trail. He'd have a hot trail on Holt, but not on Morg Mills and Trump Foster. If they could have the robbery and the killings pinned on Holt they'd be in the clear. But there was one thing Holt was sure of now. They'd have to kill him to make him keep his mouth shut, in case he might be able to prove that he had had nothing to do with the robbery and the killings.

Holt ground-reined the sorrel a half a mile from the camp, took his Winchester, then padded through the sunlit glades until he could look down upon the camp. Cass Riker was seated on a log, trying to repair one of his boots. There was no sign of anyone else near the camp. Holt whistled softly.

"It's me, Old Whiskers," said Holt.

"Where the hell you been? To a soiree or somethin'?"

"Get your horse. Lead him around this ridge. Get moving. I got news for you, Pop."

"What's up?" he asked.

Holt swiftly explained what had happened in Yardigan, but he eliminated the fact that Stuart had been looking for one Holt Deaver, suspect in the robbery and killing at Fort Mohave. Holt didn't want the old badger to have anything on him. Not yet anyway. Not until Cass led the way to his hidden loot.

They rode slowly toward the north, intending to circle Yardigan and then head up into the canyons toward Horse Mountain. The sun slanted down through the treetops to heat the ground and the resinous odor of the pines mingled with that of the dry wind that swept up from the desert.

"Shoulda got me a smarter partner," said Cass Riker sourly. "You run right into them boys! Blast and damn anyway!"

Holt drew rein sharply and leaned toward Riker. "Listen," he said harshly. "I helped you back there at Alamo Springs. If I hadn't, they would have been still working over you to make you talk. I got you through that desert and now I'm taking you through these mountains. If I ride off and leave you here, you'll get lost in an hour. Now you shut up that flapping mouth of yours or I'll let you go it alone!"

"And you lose ten thousand bucks, eh? You loco fool!"

Holt smashed a fist down on his pommel. "You and your damned ten thousand bucks! I don't believe you ever had more than the ten dollars you got as a parting gift from Yuma Pen!"

"Go on thenl Leave! In a week I'll be lightin' seegars with hundred dollar bills, and laughing fit to bust my belly thinking of you eatin' beans and bacon in the mountains."

Holt kept a check on his raging temper. He couldn't go back. Not now. He was shackled to the old man and he would have to stay that way until he knew whether or not the old coot was lying in his dirty beard.

"Straightened you out, didn't it?" jeered Riker.

Something made Holt turn in his saddle. Far down the slope the sun glinted on metal. There was a movement in amongst the trees and he saw a horseman leave the woods and then look up the tree-stippled slope of the mountain toward the two fugitives. Then he turned in his saddle, took off his hat and waved it to someone unseen.

There were no more hot words between Holt Deaver and Cass Riker. They spurred up the slope, heading for a notch. Whoever it was down there was probably no friend to them. Right now it seemed as though every man's hand was against those two.

4

THEY had crossed the Verde River an hour before dusk the day after they had left the Yardigan area. Holt still hadn't been able to worm any information out of Cass Riker as to where their journey would end. The old man was as close-mouthed as a clam, and the further into the mountains they went, the more concerned Holt became. He was getting no closer to Sonora, and Burl Stuart had probably kept the telegraph wires hot, now that one of his suspects had high-tailed it out of Yardigan a jump and a holler ahead of Stuart.

Holt rolled a cigarette and automatically passed it on to Cass, then rolled one for himself. They halted their horses to light up. "You reckon Stuart figgered those three tarantulas was clear of that deal at Fort Mohave?" asked Cass. His sharp eyes studied Holt.

"Sure. He's got nothing on them. Besides, I told you that the bartender had told me he had seen Carley and Harris right in Yardigan not too long ago."

Cass blew out a smoke ring. "You don't suppose he told Stuart who they was?"

"He could have, to help them clear themselves of that Fort Mohave thing."

"No," said Cass quietly.

"What do you mean?"

Cass rested a hand on his cantle. "You think Stuart wouldn't have remembered those names? Everybody in Arizona knows that story. Most of them think I done away with Ernie Carley and Savvy Harris. They're still wanted for that robbery, bub. Stuart would remember them."

"So they gave him phoney names?"

"Yeh, and unless that barkeep opens his mouth I don't think Stuart could have been any the wiser."

"That barkeep is smart enough to keep his mouth shut, Cass. He wouldn't want two hardcases like Carley and Harris down on him."

"Yup."

They rode on toward the east and then suddenly Cass turned to eye Holt. "You never did tell what you was runnin' from, bub."

"What makes you so sure I'm running from something?"

Cass grinned wickedly. "I got ways of figgering things out."

"You sure do, and most of them wrong."

"I wonder who that was we seen when we was climbing that mountain?"

"*Quien sabe?* Could have been your old *compadres*."

"Or the boys that been chasing you."

"There you go again!"

Riker's gimlet eyes probed into Holt's eyes. "Sure are a mysterious little fella, ain'tcha?"

Holt ignored the old man. He drew rein. "I'm backtrailing."

"Why?"

"To see if we're being followed. You keep on going. Head for that pinnacle of rock you can see due east. I'll be along soon."

"You'd better be."

Holt waved a hand and then trotted back along the trail. He was getting used to riding bareback, but he sure wished he had left his old saddle on his horse. Maybe Foster and Mills had found that saddle and had known he had made Alamo Springs. He wet his lips. There wasn't a chance that they had trailed Holt up into the mountains—*or was there*?

The sun was low atop the range to the west when Holt halted, slid from his horse, then led him into cover. He took his rifle and padded back along the trail until he could see the narrow Verde flowing lazily between its banks with the late afternoon sun glinting from the clear waters.

Then he saw the movement in the trees a hundred yards back from the far bank of the river. A horseman, riding slowly, with rifle across his thighs, while he looked to right and left through the woods. A moment later another horseman appeared. Holt felt a sickening feeling in the pit of his stomach. He needed no fieldglasses to recognize *those* two men. The big, broad-shouldered man in the lead was Trump Foster, wearing his usual cowhide vest and yellowish hat. The other man was Morg Mills, lean and deadly looking, dressed all in gray.

Holt lay still, hardly daring to breathe, while the two men stopped their horses on the far bank and looked across the rippling waters to the bank where Holt was hidden. He could have sworn that Morg Mills was looking directly at him.

There was no chance for him to pull out of there now. If they crossed the river ford, they'd pass within twenty feet of him, and if his horse whinnied there'd be hell to pay.

"This is as good a place as any, Morg," said Trump Foster.

The tall man nodded. He dismounted and led his bay to the water's edge to let it drink, but all the time his eyes flicked through the greenery of the opposite shore. The wind was blowing straight

55

down the valley. If it shifted and the horses scented each other, Holt might have to get out of there two spits and a jump ahead of singing lead.

The big man began to undo his cantle pack. "I figger we'd better forget him, Morg. We keep foolin' around in this country and we might get picked up. You remember what them fellas said back there at Yardigan? That marshal is after Holt Deaver. He ain't after *us*. Right now he ain't anyways. I say we ought to go back and get the money we cached and take off for Sonora and to hell with Holt Deaver."

Morg turned slowly and took the cigarette from his mouth. "You forget one thing, Trump."

"So?"

"He *killed* my brother."

Trump nodded. "Well, maybe we oughta shut him up permanent-like. Why didn't the loco cuss throw in with us?"

"Deaver never did like killing."

Trump spat. "He does a good chore of it when he does. He gunned Mike down so fast it damned near threw me too. That's how he made his break. Then there was that *hombre* he killed back at Alamo Springs. What was his name?"

"Harris. Webb Harris."

"Yeh, the kid brother to that tough-looking galoot Savvy." Trump squatted by his blankets and began to fashion a smoke. "Quite a brother killer, ain't he?"

"Shut up!"

"All right, Morg. Take it easy. I didn't mean nothing."

"You never do."

Trump lighted his smoke. "You still think Deaver is with that old bastard Riker?"

"That's him we saw with Deaver yesterday when they climbed Horse Mountain."

Trump blew a smoke ring. "What the hell are Carley, Shalen, and Harris trailing Riker for?"

Morg traced a pattern on the ground with a stick. "Riker, Harris, Carley and Shalen were all in on the big haul fifteen years ago with the *dinero*. Later on he got caught. No one ever found out what happened to the others. Lot of people thought Riker had done away with 'em. I knew better. I saw Carley down in Sonora some years ago. He didn't tell me, but I got the idea that he and the others were waiting for Riker to get sprung out of Yuma so they could find out where he cached the *dinero*."

Trump whistled softly. "You suppose that's why Deaver is with Riker?"

"He threw in with him back at Alamo Springs, didn't he?"

Trump nodded. "How much loot did Riker get away with?"

"Hundred and twenty thousand, Trump."

Holt stared at the man. The amount got higher every time it got talked about.

"No wonder them three *hombres* are after Riker."

Morg nodded. He stood up and looked across the river. "One hundred and twenty thousand bucks! And we profited by a measly twelve thousand back there on the Colorado. Six thousand lousy bucks!"

Trump shrugged. "I ain't kickin', Morg."

The tall man turned savagely. "No, you wouldn't! You've always been a tinhorn, penny-ante cuss! You can't think big! Supposing we could get our hands on that *dinero* Riker salted away? Sixty thousand dollars apiece, Trump! Sixty thousand dollars!"

"Sixty-six thousand. You forget the payroll money."

Morg squatted beside Trump. "Maybe we could throw in with Carley, Harris and Shalen and give them a hand in running down Deaver and Riker?"

"Hell! That'd cut down the profits, Morg. You divide a hundred and twenty thousand by five and you get only twenty-four thousand apiece."

"A little while ago you were satisfied with six thousand."

Trump flipped his cigarette butt into the river. "Sure, but that was before you got me to thinking." He looked sideways at Morg. "Supposing we did throw in with them? Until we got our hands on that *dinero*. Ain't nothing stopping us from getting rid of them like we done those soldiers at the Colorado."

Morg grinned. "Now, you're talking, Trump!"

Half an hour drifted past and darkness was creeping down into the valley of the Verde when three more horsemen rode up to the campfire beside the Verde. Ernie Carley, Savvy Harris and Pete Shalen. The wind had shifted and the fire crackled, so it was impossible for Holt to hear what they were saying. There was one thing he did know. He had to slow them down. He'd have to take a long chance, for the five of them were as tough a set of hardcases as ever were seen in Arizona Territory, a place noted for such local products.

Holt wriggled back from his lookout and bellied across the open ground to a rock formation. He slid his rifle across the top of it. He had twelve rounds in the magazine. Enough to raise a little hell across the river.

He wet his lips. The five of them were seated, or lying around the campfire, talking in low voices. Beyond the camp the five horses had been tethered to trees.

It would be so easy to drive a slug into one of them and then get at least two more of them before they could break away from the firelight. Who would it be first? It wasn't in him to kill men from ambush, yet he knew any one of the five of them probably wouldn't give a second thought about killing Holt the same way.

He sighted carefully and squeezed off. The forty-four slug struck the big coffee pot that rested beside the fire, smashing it, scattering hot coffee over the men about the fire. They leaped to their feet as the echo of the shot slammed back and forth in the valley of the Verde. They were etched against the bright light. Holt fired again and heard a horse scream in pain and fear. It had been almost as difficult as shooting at a man, but he had to slow those hardcases down.

He fired three more times before one of the yelling men doused the fire with water. The gun flashes dotted the darkness like rubies on velvet and the hungry slugs whipped through the brush not too far from Holt. A horse broke loose and splashed across the river. Holt stood up and pumped his Winchester dry in the general direction of the camp, then grabbed the runaway and swung up into the saddle, slashing at him with the gun barrel.

The moon was just rising when he reached the high land to the east of the Verde. He grinned as he heard an occasional shot. The boys had been pinned down for a little while at least. He rode toward the naked pinnacle of rock that thrust itself up from the ground like an admonishing finger. The old man would be wondering what had happened to him.

The moon lighted the valley of the Verde when Holt reached the rock pinnacle. There was no sign of Cass Riker. Holt rode back and forth, whistling softly. But Cass Riker had vanished like a ghost into the wilderness.

Old Cass had played it smart, getting Holt to save his skin back at Alamo Springs, having him guide the way through desert and mountains, and having him risk arrest by going into Yardigan for supplies. Now the old coot knew the rest of the way and a double-damned fool had gone back to hold off their pursuers while he had skinned out as free as a bird. He had most of the supplies, too.

There was one thing Holt had a good share of though; he had plenty of forty-fours for both Winchester and Colt. The old goat owed him ten thousand dollars, or at least enough money to get him safely to Sonora, and Holt Deaver meant to cash in his six-gun against the old buzzard's head for that *dinero*.

The valley of the Verde was quiet now and the moon glinted on the shallow waters as they purled and rippled along. The wind shifted a little and brought the odor of wet burned wood. Holt reloaded his Winchester, then touched the big buckskin with his spurs. He rode to the east. He really didn't know why, but instinct told him that was the way Cass Riker had gone.

To the east was the Mogollon Rim and the Mogollon Plateau, still haunted by Apaches, the real rimrock boys who hadn't yet been subjugated by the army. Old Cass would take his life in his hands going in there. It was a chance Holt had to take too. He couldn't go back to the west. Those five hardcases were back there and so was Burl Stuart. There were too many settlements to the north and they'd be looking for Holt Deaver after Burl Stuart had spread the good word. To the south was rough country and Holt wasn't ready yet to go that way.

It was going to be a long ride but there might be ten thousand dollars at the end of it. Or maybe death in a Tonto ambush. High, low or jack, Holt Deaver was on his way, and God help the old man when Holt caught up with him.

5

THE night wind blew down from Mazatzal Peak and whispered strange forebodings to Holt Deaver as he led the two horses across a small mesa. The moon flooded the country with pure, silvery light by which a man could look for Apaches making damned sure they didn't see him first. They didn't attack at night, or they'd never get into the House of Spirits if they were killed, but they had the patience of spiders and would trail a man for miles, especially a man armed with a fine handgun and a long gun, and two good horses.

Holt wanted to stay holed up until the moon died, but he couldn't take a chance on that. Those five men back at the Verde were just as cruel and vicious as any Apaches, and a lot more capable. Holt had taken care of at least two of their horses, but that had left three mounts, and he knew well enough that those three horses would be used to follow him.

Even after the moon died he'd have to keep on, for he knew he couldn't travel during daylight hours in Tonto country. The big war bands had long ago been subjugated, but there were plenty of broncho Apaches still on the loose, and a lone white man with weapons and two fine horses would be fair game for them. Maybe they'd get Cass Riker too and then no one would ever know where his money, however much it was, could be found.

Somewhere off to the south a coyote howled dismally. A moment later another coyote gave voice to the north, almost as though he was answering right over Holt's head. It wasn't until he was at the east end of the mesa, looking down into a dark canyon, like a trough of ink in the ground, that he heard the third coyote calling from the east, and he knew well enough that those weren't coyotes talking back and forth out there. They were Apaches.

He led the two horses down a long slope, hoping to God that their noise wouldn't give him away. Their shod hoofs struck bright little sparks from the stones, and the cold sweat of fear ran down Holt's body and soaked his shirt, chilling him when the wind blew against him.

He had enough at last. He picketed the horses in a draw on the sloping canyon wall, then walked a quarter of a mile up the canyon until he found a place where he could hide and get some sleep. He wanted a smoke desperately, but those keen noses out there would pick up the blessed odor of the burning weed and travel down it until they found Holt Deaver, and the next smoke he would inhale would be that of brimstone and pitch in the nether regions.

There was no use in driving on through the night with hate as the spur. Holt had to use his head. He had been outsmarted just as Riker had outsmarted Carley, Shalen and Harris. Riker used anyone who got in his clutches. He knew how to play on a man's greed all right. He had plenty of greed himself for that matter. One hundred and twenty thousand dollars was a lot of *dinero* for one old rascal to play around with. Ten thousand of that was Holt's and now he meant to get it.

It was still dark when he awoke. He raised his head and sniffed the night wind, almost as though it could warn him about his enemies. And he had a lot of them now.

He stood up and picked up his rifle, then crawled out of the hollow to go for his horses. It was so dark he could hardly see the ground to make his way and when he reached the place where he had left the horses he couldn't see, hear or smell them. He rubbed his jaws. They *had* to be there! He had picketed them well enough. One of them might have broken loose, but not *two* of them. Then a cold and evil thought crept into his mind like a worm. He knew well enough they could not have broken loose. Someone had loosed them and driven them off.

He crouched down and looked low

across the ground, trying to skyline anyone who might be in the area; he saw nothing but the brush and the rock formations. Slowly he scanned the area and as he did so some of his old scouting skill came back to him. He had been careless in the days since he had left scouting for owlhooting. A man might very well be so in breaking the law, but no man could be negligent in hostile Apache country and live to boast about it.

Holt worked his way down the slope and looked down into the canyon. It was pitch black down there but he knew he had to plunge into that evil ink in order to cross the canyon and gain the heights on the far side. If he was caught on this side of the canyon when daylight came, he'd never have a chance to cross. He had no food and just half a canteen of water, for he had left his big canteen with Cass Riker.

Then an icy calm came over him as he reached the bottom of the canyon and he was no longer afraid. He was halfway across the canyon floor when his eyes picked out a humped shape directly in front of him. For a long moment he stared at it and then he knew what it was. A horse or mule. He moved a little closer and saw that it was a horse, with its throat cut. Then he saw where the flanks and more tender cuts of meat had been sliced from the carcass. It was then that he recognized the horse. It was the sorrel, his own faithful horse.

Holt's hands tightened on his rifle and a sheer flood of hate and killing lust poured over him. Now he was no longer purely concerned with escaping from the Tontos. He wanted them to pay for his fear and what they had done to his horse. It was better for it to have died back there at Alamo Springs after faithfully carrying his master there, rather than to be degraded in death like this.

He padded across the canyon floor and made his way halfway up the slope, then stopped to look and listen. The night brought him nothing but the usual sounds: the dry husking of the wind through the trough of the canyon; the scuttling of nocturnal animals in the brush; the far-off crying of coyotes.

Every fiber in him seemed to cry for him to take off as fast as he could go, to be out of that country before the gray light of dawn, but the hate and determination within him was stronger than that. It was almost as though he was two men instead of one, and the one that wanted vengeance was the one that won out.

As he climbed the canyon wall he found a narrow, winding trail that slanted at an angle toward the top. He did not follow it. More than one white man had died just that way. Apaches knew they tended to follow trails and camp as near to water as possible and they set their ambushes accordingly. He made his way up the steep wall of the canyon, then found a place where he could hide and still see the place where the trail reached the top of the canyon. They might not come this way, but if they did . . .

He counted his cartridges and made sure his rifle magazine was full. He checked his Colt and loosened his sheath knife. He allowed himself a mouthful of water and half a handful of cigarette tobacco which he chewed with relish.

Hour after hour he squatted there, a lean lath of a man with a face as hard as flint and with cold death in his gray eyes, until the first faint traces of the false dawn tinged the eastern sky and a cold searching wind swept across the Mogollon Plateau.

He touched his dry lips with the tip of his tongue and hefted his Winchester. Then, as the wind shifted, he heard a faint sound from below the canyon rim. He moved noiselessly, shifting until he could see the place where the trail met the canyon rim. Anyone coming up the trail would be clearly silhouetted there.

Then suddenly as though manipulated by the almost invisible strings of a giant master of marionettes, a mounted figure reached the brink of the canyon, and there was no mistaking his race. The thick mane of hair bound tightly about the forehead with a band of cloth. The naked upper body and the buckskin kilt. The thigh-length, button-toed moccasins turned down about the knotty calves.

One after the other they rose out of the cold depths of the canyon until seven of them were riding right across Holt's field of fire. For a moment he hesitated and the killing fever waned a little, until he saw that the last warrior was leading a saddled horse; the big buckskin Holt had captured at the Verde, and hanging from the saddle were strips and joints of meat. There wasn't any doubt in his mind as to where that meat had been procured.

They had stolen his buckskin and they had killed his sorrel, and they would have killed him too had they been able to find him. Perhaps, if they had had time, they would have played with him, keeping him alive as long as possible for their cold amusement. He had seen some of their work when he had been a scout.

He raised the rifle, sighted calmly on the broad chest of the last brave, then squeezed off the trigger before he had time to reconsider his drastic action. The big slug smashed the warrior back and he slid lifelessly from the back of his calico horse. The first echo had hardly started racing across the canyon when the second shot ripped out and the lead buck went down with a smashed shoulder.

The warriors had little chance now as long as Holt could shoot and as long as he had them panicked. His third, fourth, and fifth shots brought down another buck and two horses. The horses thrashed about and a hoof caught another warrior in the chest, driving him down to die before he could find shelter or reply to Holt's crashing Winchester.

The smoke drifted about the screaming, struggling Apaches, while the soft-nosed forty-fours drove through the smoke and sought flesh until the Winchester clicked dryly.

Then Holt Deaver drew out his Colt, and swiftly reloaded the hot rifle, while watching for an attack. One man did come, racing silently over the rough ground, through the rifting smoke, and the two white bands of clay across his nose and upper cheeks gave him the look of a demon straight from hell. He launched himself from a rock, knife in hand, and was met by two belly shots that killed him before he hit the ground.

Holt finished loading the Winchester and left his hideout, walking coldly and deliberately toward the bloody havoc he had caused. He had no way of knowing whether or not the party he had attacked was all the Apaches in that area. He had one advantage if there were more of them, they'd stay away from that ambush after death claimed all of their mates.

Five more shots killed wounded horses, leaving Holt with the big buckskin. The buckskin was frightened until Holt spoke quietly to him and he could smell white man odor instead of Apache.

There was food amongst the scattered bags lying about on the ground. There was even a bottle of good Baconora mezcal, and Holt needed that worse than he did food.

It was quiet now that death had taken

over on the mesa. The wind whispered across the canyon and an intense loneliness took over. Holt led the horse to the east. A lone warrior lay beside the trail, face downward, with a knife still clutched in his right hand. He was in a hurry, for he had to make tracks out of that place of death.

It was then that the buck came up off the ground like an uncoiling spring, and he struck hard and viciously for Holt's belly, the honed tip of the blade taking a long cut through jacket, shirt and undershirt, barely scoring the lean belly, but it was enough to make Holt wince in pain and bend down in a reflex action. The return swipe caught him to the left of his nose, tracing a hot course across the cheekbone, through the cheek and down across the lower jaw. A deluge of blood spurted out as Holt managed enough strength to lift the steel-shod butt of the Winchester and strike the brave atop the head, smashing his skull.

Holt grunted in savage pain. The blood

poured from his bashed face, and he tried to stanch it with his bandana.

"Damned fool!" he raged at himself. "Double-damned fool!"

He should have known better but it was too late now. Another inch or two in that first slash and he would have been disemboweled. Now he'd carry a livid scar on his lean face for the rest of his life, permanent reminder to him for the rest of his life that you can't take chances with these Indians.

He led the buckskin to the east, holding to the reins with his right hand, while keeping the bandana tightly against the wound. A slow thirst crept up into his throat. He had experienced that before when wounded. It wouldn't make it any easier on him in that hellhole of heat, tangled shrubbery and lost canyons. But there was no way back now for Holt Deaver. He was committed again to the long ride.

Even as he slogged along the mesa atop in the first rays of the rising sun the buzzards began to gather like scraps of charred paper floating up there. They'd watch and wait for they were arrant cowards. But they had plenty of time and they knew there was plenty of fresh meat on which to gorge themselves, and after that, well there was the lone human and his big horse heading into death country. They'd find him when his time came.

6

HE had made it to a large sheltered basin before the fever overtook him. He had tried to cleanse the wound with mezcal, and had fortified himself additionally by drinking some of the strong liquor, but it hadn't helped his light-headedness at all. Holt made his camp in a cave overlooking the basin, after picketing his horse in a hidden place beside a trickling branch of the stream which watered the basin.

The intense loneliness of the place preyed on his mind, the fever took final hold and in his delirium he saw again people and events of the past.

Suddenly an unearthly scream threaded eerily through the quiet canyon. Cold sweat broke out on him before he realized it was the hunting cry of a mountain lion. This was their stronghold and their domain. You rarely ever saw them but they were always there. You'd see tracks of them and hear their screaming at night, but rare indeed was the man who could say he had seen one.

Holt sat up and wiped the sweat from his face. The bandage was clotted thickly to the slashed flesh of his face and there was a throbbing beneath the bandage. The flesh had puffed up so that his left eye was almost closed. His throat was dry and harsh as though it had been thoroughly sanded. He sipped a little water and crawled to the mouth of the cave. He lay there a long time before he again heard the cry of the lion.

Then he stood up and reached for his rifle. The lion was prowling about the area where his horse was picketed. The big buckskin would be frantic with fright.

Holt walked unsteadily down the slope and through the brush and trees, following the course of the stream, trying to see clearly with his one eye. His head pounded and throbbed like a tom-tom.

He stopped several hundred yards from where he had left the horse. The wind was blowing toward him, so the lion would not scent him. Now it was quiet again except for the soughing of the wind through the trees and the soft murmuring of the stream.

Then the lion struck, driving down on the frightened buckskin with full weight, crushing him down and killing him with swift skill. The buckskin had made one little whinny and the sound was followed by that of thrashing hoofs and the low growling of the killer.

Holt ran forward, raising his rifle for the shot. The lion heard him, turned, crouched, worked his hind legs, then sped forward like a stone hurled from a sling, rising from the ground. The moonlight showed the big beast clearly and Holt fired twice from the hip. The big slugs ripped into the cat but the impetus of its drive carried it forward to strike Holt fully and drive him back into the stream, while the claws, in a last convulsive effort, ripped through Holt's already ragged clothing and played final havoc with it. The tips of the claws raked his chest and belly until the cat was past him and kicking spasmodically in the final throes.

The cold water flowed over Holt's body as he struggled up. The last of the gunshots was still echoing faintly down the long canyon to the west of the basin, far enough to awaken five men who had camped beside the stream.

Holt got to his feet, feeling the hot blood run down mingling with the cold water. He looked at the dead cat, half awash in the stream, then spat thickly upon the carcass.

He walked to the horse and looked down upon it. There'd be no riding out of that canyon for Holt Deaver. What he had feared had happened.

There was nothing to be done. He had his food and ammunition up at the cave. He turned on a heel and walked through the swaying brush beneath the stark shadows of the trees making his way up the slope. Then he entered the cave and peeled off jacket, shirt and undershirt to look at his raked flesh. The claws would be filthy, as they always were, and infection a sure thing. In his weakened condition it might mean death. He had to get out of there right now and head for a settlement and medical care, no matter what would happen to him there. Prison would be better than ending his days in screaming torment in a forgotten canyon, facing death utterly alone.

He bathed the wounds with mezcal, then emptied the last strong liquor into his mouth, gasping a little with the ripe stinging of it, and in a little while its strength became his strength, and he left the cave, walking slowly but steadily to the east through the naked moonlight, like a man in a hazy dream.

Far behind Holt Deaver the five men who had heard the shooting had already saddled up, and were riding along the stream, heading east along the canyon as Holt Deaver was heading, and they rode with their rifles across their thighs, while the last of the five led a laden burro.

The boy had found the stray and had roped him to bring him back to the little ranch further up the big forked canyon when something made him turn his head, and as he did so his hand dropped to the old Colt which hung holstered at his thigh. He swallowed hard as he stared at the apparition which stood on the far side of the stream staring back at him. A lean lath of a man, wearing tattered, blood-stained clothing, with a filthy and bloody bandage swathing the left side of his face. His toes protruded from the wrecks of boots he wore, and he leaned on a Winchester rifle.

The man opened his mouth and closed it, as though he wanted to speak and could not.

The boy kneed his mare away from the edge of the stream and eased his Colt free from the holster.

The man tried to speak again, raised a hand weakly, then fell face forward into the stream and lay still. The boy slid from his mare and waded into the stream. He hauled the man partway up on the bank and rolled him over. The man opened his eyes, smiled weakly and then said,

"*Gracias*." His head lolled to one side and he passed out again.

The boy splashed across the stream and swung up on his mare. He rode swiftly toward the big fork of the canyon with the stray pounding along behind him.

His dreams were peopled again, but this time the actors were different. A freckled boy of about fourteen or fifteen, and a young woman, perhaps of twenty years of age, with dark hair and lovely hazel eyes and hands like healing instruments. Then there was the broth and the strong tea. The bathings and the fresh bandages. The warm, soft bed and the crackling of the fire at night, casting strange shadows on the ceiling of the room and the chinked log walls.

But he was alive and the fever had been broken, leaving him as weak as a new born babe. He looked at his gaunt hands and hardly recognized them. He closed his eyes a little again and saw the young woman poking up the fire. She wore a neat gingham dress, and her long dark hair had been caught up with a bright green ribbon at the base of her shapely neck. He closed his eyes as she turned and came back to the table. Then he felt a wondrously cool hand on his hot forehead and he knew she was not a dream.

Holt opened his eyes. "Hello," he said in a dry voice.

She smiled. "Hello," she answered. "It's been a long time for you, hasn't it?"

"How long?"

"Three days."

"Lost forever."

She nodded. "Your wounds were an awful mess. How did you get them?"

"Mountain lion."

She nodded again, but there was a faint look of suspicion in her lovely hazel eyes. "You'll be all right in a few days. What happened to you might have killed many another man. You're all rawhide and steel springs, so my brother says." She flushed a little as she turned to measure out some medicine into a glass.

"Not much rawhide and steel left in me," he said quietly.

"Where have you come from?"

There was no use in lying. "From the Verde."

The spoon clattered against the glass. She turned and looked down upon him with disbelief on her face. "You must have flown then."

He raised his feet a little and wiggled them. "No," he said. "Partway on a horse and the rest of the way on shank's mare. A lion killed my horse and I killed the lion, but he got a few last licks in on me."

She studied him. "I almost believe you," she said at last.

"Why don't you believe me fully?"

"Do you know where you are?"

He shrugged, wincing as the bandages on his belly and chest drew against the healing flesh. "No."

"You're on the East Fork of the Bandera."

It was his turn to stare at her in disbelief. "How did I get this far?"

She handed him the glass. "You must have walked here after your horse was killed."

"You mean you *found* me *here?*"

"My brother Tim did, but you were only two miles from this house. You must have come through the mountain country west of here if you came from the Verde. Do you know how far that is?"

"It doesn't matter. I won't believe it."

"Over sixty miles," she said quietly. "Another thing: The Tontos have been raiding all around that country. A white man couldn't get through that country. Alone anyway. He'd need at least a company of cavalry with him."

"Aren't *you* afraid of them?"

She shook her head. "They won't bother us."

"You're sure of that?"

"Positive," she said quietly.

He closed his eyes. "Meaning you're too close to a settlement or an army post?"

"No. Why do you ask?"

"Why should they let you alone then?"

"I'll tell you later." She placed a hand on his forehead.

"Is he all right now?" a boyish voice asked from the doorway.

"His fever has broken, Tim."

Holt opened his eyes and looked at the boy. "Hello Tim," he said. "Thanks for helping me."

The boy smiled. "You sure scared me. You looked like Rip Van Winkle standing there."

"Tim!" his sister protested.

Holt grinned. "He's probably right."

She smoothed his pillow. "I'm Susan Morris and this is my brother Timothy."

"*Tim!*" the boy said.

"Tim is all right with me," said Holt.

"You haven't told us your name," she said.

He hesitated. He'd have to take a chance, for he might have talked in his delirium. "Holt Deaver," he said.

Tim stared at him. "Sis," he said, "this is the man Uncle Cass spoke about!"

A cold feeling broke out in Holt, and his hands gripped the edge of the coverlet. "Uncle Cass?" he asked quietly.

"Sure! You know Uncle Cass! He talked a lot about you, Mister Deaver!"

"Yeh, I know Uncle Cass. Where is he?"

"He only stayed here one night and then he left on business. Said he'd be back in about a week or ten days. Went south, he did."

"On *business*?"

"Yes," said the boy proudly, "and he said we'd never have to worry about money no more, 'cause he was going to take care of us from now on, on account of us bein' orphans. Said he'd send me to school anywhere I wanted to go. I didn't like *that* so much, but he also promised me a silver mounted Winchester and a new saddle."

Holt glanced at the girl. "How long since you saw Uncle Cass?" he asked casually.

"You mean before he came here?"

"Yes."

She turned a little. "How long has it been, Tim? You were a baby then, hardly a few months old. Fifteen years ago I think it was. I was only a child. I could just about remember him."

"Fifteen years would be just about right," said Holt dryly. "What did he say about me?"

Tim came to stand beside the bed. "He said to give you the best of everything until he got back. He said he owed you a debt."

Holt nodded. He remembered the night he had held off the five outlaws back at the Verde only to find out that Cass Riker had vanished like wind driven smoke.

Susan smiled. "He said he didn't think you'd make it, but if you did, you were to have the best of everything. We haven't much, Mister Deaver, but what we have is yours."

He looked about the comfortable room, neat and clean, and then he smiled at her. "To a man like me, Miss Morris, this room itself is enough, and your care is all the reward I ever want."

She flushed a little. "We would have done it for anyone, Mister Deaver. I have some nursing skill. My father was a doctor, formerly a contract surgeon at Fort Apache, and he became interested in treating the Apaches. I can tell you that we are considered their friends. That is why they let us live here, and have done so since Father died two years ago."

"And now Uncle Cass has come back to help you?"

She smiled. "Yes. Isn't it wonderful?"

He nodded. "I suppose you heard from Uncle Cass before he returned?"

She shook her head. "We never knew where he was. I had heard he was in Mexico and had some kind of business down there. My father rarely spoke of him. You see, Uncle Cass was my mother's younger brother, and from the few stories we heard about him he was pretty wild in his younger days. But we'll forget all that now."

"Sure, sure," he said. He found it hard to look at her, knowing that her uncle was as crooked as a stake-and-rider fence. The old coot had probably figured that Holt would be wiped out back at Verde, and if he hadn't been stopped there he would never have passed through the country between the Verde and the Bandera. It was a miracle that he had passed through there with the Tontos raiding all around it. But Old Cass was no fool. He had neatly covered his trail by telling his trusting niece and nephew to expect Holt. Maybe to throw Holt off guard if he did make the Bandera.

There was one thing Holt knew for sure; he meant to be out of that bed before Old Whiskers came back to the Bandera with his saddlebags full of Wells-Fargo money. Holt meant to get his fingers into that pile of loot even if he had to drop down on the old man to do it.

"You'd better sleep now," she said.

He nodded. She snuffed out the candle that guttered on the little table. "The fire will die down soon," she said.

"Thanks, Miss Morris."

"Susan," she said with a smile.

"Susan then." He raised his head. "One thing, Susan: If anyone comes here asking for me, you never saw me."

There was a moment's silence, and then she nodded. "No," she said quietly.

"You're wondering why?"

"A little. But it didn't surprise me."

"How so?"

"Uncle Cass told me the same thing. Good night, Mister Deaver." She closed the door behind her.

He waited a few minutes, then slipped out of the bed, staggering a little in his weakness. He padded over to his gunbelt and withdrew his Colt from the sheath. He opened the loading gate and checked it. It was fully loaded. He took it back to the bed with him, sipped a glass of water, then slid the sixshooter beneath his pillow. There was nothing like Samuel Colt and Company insurance for a man like Holt Deaver.

7

THE wind was dry and brisk as it swept across the Mogollon Plateau and moved the pines, picking up their brisk resinous odor and carrying it along. The sky was dotted with fleeting clouds racing ever westward, with their shadows passing up and downhill ahead of them. A thread of smoke rose far down the forked canyon where the little ranch house and its out-buildings were hidden from view.

Holt Deaver sat Tim's mare on an escarpment, studying the land to the west through Doctor Morris' army field glasses. There was no sign of human life to the west. Nothing but a lone hawk hanging high overhead, floating on motionless wings in the strong draft of wind.

Though Holt was still weak he had forced himself from that comfortable bed after three more days of it. Old Cass still had not appeared, nor had there been any sign of the five men riding from the west. Maybe they had lost the trail, maybe . . .

Holt rolled a cigarette and lighted it, then leaned on his saddlehorn to study the country. A man, had he a mind to, could have a fine spread there. The canyon, through which the East Fork of the Bandera flowed, was well watered, protected from the heat of summer and the cold of winter, with plenty of shelter for cattle. There was timber aplenty and rock for building, if a man wanted to build well. The area was out of the way, on the very edge of Apache country, but in time they'd be under complete control, and if a railroad ran a branch line through that country, it would be easy to get in supplies and ship out fat cattle.

But there was a bitter loneliness in Holt Deaver. He was still on the run; in fact, he should have pulled out of there as soon as he was able to, but he had to wait for Old Cass and his loot. There was more to it than just that though. There was Susan

Morris. That was the bitter stab, because Holt knew he'd have to leave that country in a hurry, and he knew he'd never be able to come back again, if he was lucky enough to make Sonora.

One good thing at least was the fact that the East Fork of the Bandera was isolated from almost every other settled area within miles. Tim had told Holt that the two of them stayed at the ranch from late spring until late fall, then they moved into town where his sister worked in the small hospital as a nurse. The two of them loved the little ranch, although it hardly afforded them more than a bare living. The boy supplemented the larder by killing deer and other game. They had a small garden and a few head of cattle. But this was to have been their last year on the ranch. Tim had to get more schooling, and his sister had been willing to work to support the two of them until Tim got his education. The boy had told Holt that he wanted to be a doctor as his father had been, and he knew the long and hard road he must follow to achieve that. So they would sell the little spread for whatever they could get. It wouldn't be much, for the Tonto threat cheapened the value to anyone but the two Morrises.

He studied the country spread out beneath the escarpment. Tim had said there was plenty of land adjacent to the ranch that could be homesteaded. Good grazing land, the best range-land in that area. A good rancher could live like a king once he had put down his roots. Trouble was, Holt Deaver was a tumbleweed, with no roots.

Touching the mare with his heels, he rode down the slope. He had made himself useful about the place, suggesting some improvements such as a trough of wooden planking to bring stream water closer to the corral. He had done some rough carpentry about the place and had plastered up the huge outside chimney of the living room fireplace. He had been weak, and had worked slowly, but he had to do something to show these people he appreciated their kindness.

Reaching the canyon floor, he eyed the

rippling waters. There must be trout in that water. It was a good place. Deer, bear, fish and other game were plentiful. Cattle would thrive. Horses would flourish.

But now and then as he rode he glanced over his left shoulder at that mysterious and brooding country to the west. It was like a gigantic barrier of silence and mystery. Maybe it was haunted by other beings than the Tontos. Five of them. Maybe the Tontos had taken care of them. It would be no loss to Arizona Territory. But if those five hardcases reached the Bandera and found out that Cass Riker and Holt Deaver had reached that area, there would be gunplay along the East Fork.

Twenty-five years of life lay behind Holt Deaver. A hard life, but not reason enough for him to have turned owlhoot. Still, nothing he had ever done had been more than many another man had done in the Southwest. Sure, he had done a little rustling, some crooked gambling, and had been a hired gun several times.

But he had been a drifter, with no home to call his own, no relatives to whom he could return. A cold feeling came over him as he rode toward the ranch buildings. How long could a man go on like that?

Holt looked toward the ranch house and saw Susan feeding her chickens. The wind whipped her neat dress about her long, slim legs, and she held her dark hair back with her free hand as she fed the clucking fowls. It was a picture a man could see many times in a fire in the hidden canyons where he was forced to live until he was free of the law. If he ever got that free. But that picture would never let him be free until the day he died.

It was only after he had corraled the mare and rubbed her down that he saw the late afternoon sun glinting on something up the stream, where the rude log bridge crossed the water. Holt stepped back around the corner of the barn. Susan was walking back toward the house and then she turned and looked back toward the bridge. As she turned again she saw Holt. Their eyes met and then she looked away.

"I'll leave if you want me to," he called out.

"Why?" she asked.

"To keep you from lying."

"How do you know it's you they want?"

He did not answer for a moment. Then he shrugged. "It's logical," he said.

"What is it you have done?"

"Many things," he said dryly.

Her eyes studied him closely. "You don't have to run," she said at last. "You couldn't get far. You're not strong enough yet."

"You don't have to lie for me, Susan."

She stepped up onto the porch of the house. "I'm sorry for you, Holt," she said. "Very sorry. I won't say you are here."

Then she was gone. Holt smashed his right fist into his left palm. She had made him feel like a child caught in a wrong-doing—like an utter fool.

But there was no use in taking a chance. He walked to the rear of the barn and up the slope amongst the trees until he found a place where he was well hidden in amongst the rock ledges and brush. He quickly loaded his rifle and then squatted down behind a ledge, to watch whoever was riding toward the house. He uncased the field glasses and focused them on a point near the house. It didn't take long for the three horsemen to ride into his field of vision. They were strangers, but one of them had a star pinned to his vest.

Holt wet his dry lips as he watched them draw rein in front of the house and then dismount. Susan came out on the porch and talked with the man who wore the star. She shook her head several times. Now and then one of the men would look up and down the canyon, passing the place where Holt lay hidden.

Then the three men rode slowly back along the stream and vanished in the trees beyond the bridge. Susan went back into the house. Half an hour passed, and then

Tim came out of the house, looked up toward Holt and waved his hat.

Holt turned quickly, raising his rifle, finger on the trigger, ready to shoot and to kill. It was Susan. He lowered the rifle and let the hammer down to half-cock.

"You move like a cat," she said. "How long have you been living like this, Holt?"

He flushed a little. "Too long," he said. "Who were they?"

"Deputy Sheriff Lang Masters and two of his men."

"Who were they looking for?"

"They asked if we had seen a man on the run through here. The description matched you, Holt."

"So? It might have been someone else they were looking for."

She shook her head. "They asked for you by name."

He shoved back his hat. Then Burl Stuart had passed the notice along. They still thought he had had something to do with that mess at the Colorado. And, if anything had happened to end the lives of

Morg Mills and Trump Foster after Holt had held them back at the Verde, the whole blame for the paymaster robbery and killings would settle heavily on his shoulders. No jury would believe that he had had nothing to do with it.

She studied him. "It was about a robbery and killing near Fort Mohave," she said.

"I know," he said quietly.

"They'll eventually catch you, Holt. Wouldn't it be easier to give yourself up?"

He rolled a cigarette and lighted it. "Would you believe me if I told you that I had nothing to do with that robbery and those killings?"

She shrugged. "I don't know what to believe, Holt. If you *are* innocent why don't you turn yourself in to be cleared?"

He laughed without mirth. "It's not as easy as all that, Susan. I'm on the run, but not for killing those soldiers. I got in a gun scrape at Chloride and I might have gotten clear of that all right except for my reputation." He looked away from her as he spoke the last words.

"Is it as bad as all that?" she asked.

"It doesn't take much for a man to have a reputation in this country. I had a good one once. I served in the army as a scout. Maybe I should have stayed with them."

"Why did you leave?"

He shrugged. "I had ambitions, ideas, and they couldn't be financed with army pay. I tried a few things, then drifted along until it was easy to break the law. There is one thing you must believe though: I am not a killer."

"But you have killed men?"

"Yes. But it has never been murder, Susan. Those soldiers were killed by two men I knew. I was forced to kill the brother of one of them to escape from them, or they would have killed me to keep my mouth shut. I ran. Maybe that was a mistake, but a man doesn't think clearly at times like that. I killed another man. I dropped his horse and he was killed in the fall."

"You make it sound so innocent."

He dropped his cigarette and stamped on it. "You see?" he demanded. "What chance does a man have to explain once they daub him with the tar brush?"

"You can turn yourself in, Holt."

He shook his head. "No, not until I see your uncle."

Their eyes met and she came closer to him. "What do you have to do with him, Holt?"

He looked away. "It was a business deal."

"What *kind* of business?"

"It has nothing to do with you, Susan." He picked up his rifle. "I'll be pulling out of here tonight," he said. "You can loan me a horse. I'll leave it where Timmie can pick it up."

"Running again?"

"Yes," he said fiercely. "You don't know why! It isn't your way of life! What do you know about men like me? Let me leave here and you'll never be bothered by me again."

She eyed his taut face and the healing scar; the gaunt look of this tired wolf of a man, and her heart could not help but go out to him. "Stay awhile, Holt," she said quietly. "You'll be safe here until you decide to leave." She walked to the far end of the barn and then turned. "We'll eat in twenty minutes. There'll be hot biscuits and venison too." Then she was gone.

He yanked off his hat and slammed it on the ground. Curse the blasted fates that drove a man like him on and on even after he had decided to leave his way of life and try to reform. The desire was within him all right, and he knew he could do it, but the world wouldn't let him go that easily. He was tabbed and marked, and wherever he went his reputation would follow him. It was a marked deck for men like Holt Deaver.

The sickening thing about it all was something that had slowly moved into his mind in the past two days. It was Susan Morris. He had known many women of all kinds, but he had never been fool enough to fall in love; with his way of life it would never pan out. Now, while in the biggest mess of his life, he had the luck to fall in love.

He picked up hat and rifle and walked toward the house. Somewhere along the distant escarpment a coyote howled, and the utter loneliness of that haunting cry cut into Holt Deaver like the bite of a whiplash, for it was a loneliness akin to his own.

8

THERE was no use in him trying to sleep. The thoughts that teemed through his mind drove all sleep away. Holt got up from the bed where he had dropped fully clothed some hours before. He walked to the window and looked out toward the murmuring stream. The moon was on the wane but it was still clear enough to see distant objects, and as he felt for the makings he saw a movement down near the bridge. He eyed the man who was riding slowly along the bank of the stream and then he saw the ragged beard, ruffled by the night wind.

Holt reached for his gunbelt and swung it about his lean hips, buckling it swiftly and settling it. He placed his hat on his head and then quietly left the room. The house was silent, and only a few coals showed in the bed of ashes in the huge fireplace. He slipped out of the back door and edged his way around the side of the house farthest away from the direction from which Cass Riker was approaching.

He had made it just in time, for Riker had dismounted in front of the house and was loosening the girth of his saddle. Holt crossed the patch of ground between them with silent strides, but even so Cass whirled, and his hand dropped to his Colt only for him to see Holt's sixshooter at belly level, and to look into cold gray eyes.

Riker smiled uneasily. "Howdy, bub," he said.

Holt nodded.

Riker tilted his head to one side. "Some filly give you a gouge in the face for gettin' too fresh?"

Holt shook his head.

"Talkative cuss, ain'tcha?"

"Where's the money, Riker?"

Riker grinned. "Oh, *that*?"

"Yeh . . . *that*."

"I ain't got it with me, bub."

The Colt muzzle touched Riker's navel.

"Where is it, Old Whiskers?" asked Holt coldly.

Riker slowly reached up and scratched in his disreputable beard. "Cached," he said.

"Same place, I suppose?"

"No. I moved it."

"Why didn't you bring it back here? Your niece and nephew been expecting it, *Uncle* Cass. They said they'd never have to worry about money any more, 'cause Uncle Cass was going to take care of them. High class schooling, a silver mounted Winchester and a new saddle for Timmie. Maybe a rich husband for Susan."

Riker's face darkened. "You talk a helluva lot, bub."

"Not as much as you're going to talk, Old Whiskers."

"I told them to look out for you!"

"Sure, after you jumped up a hell of a lot of dust leaving me behind at the Verde to pull your damned chestnuts out of the fire."

Riker tilted his head. "So you stopped them there anyways?"

"You damned tooting I did!"

"Well, you should have killed them."

"You cold-gutted shark! You don't give a damn who I kill just so long as you keep your shirttail clean, do you? Now, where's that money? I never expected to dun you for that ten thousand bucks, Old Whiskers, but I'm doing it now."

Riker shrugged. "It ain't here, bub."

"Step back!"

Riker obliged.

"Now open those saddlebags and dump them out on the ground!

The old man shrugged. He unbuckled the bags, opened them and dumped the contents onto the moonlit ground. Holt poked a boot toe amongst the things. An extra shirt, undershirt, a filthy towel, and the usual odds and ends a man would ordinarily carry in saddlebags. Holt eyed the old man. "Peel," he said shortly.

"You double-dammed fool! You think I got all that money on me?" Riker slapped his thighs and his sides. "Look! Or has that scar ruined your eyesight?"

There wasn't any doubt but that the old coot was telling the truth. Holt gripped Riker by the front of the shirt and drew him close. "I'm going to take you out into the barn, Old Whiskers, and pound the truth outa you!"

Riker smirked a little. "Now, bub, take it easy! Lemme tell you what happened."

Riker straightened his shirt as Holt released him. "I seen your old *compadres* at the West Fork of the Bandera. They was camped there. I durned near run into 'em. Sure, I had the *dinero* with me! But I wasn't about to take any chances on them finding me with it, so I cached it."

"Seems like I heard this one before."

"You still think I'm trying to euchre you outa that money I promised you?"

"I haven't seen any money, Riker. I don't even know if you have any money at all. All I know is that if I hadn't showed up to help you, and got you as far as the Verde, you'd be in the hands of those three boys of yours, and if they

113

hadn't squeezed the information out of you as to where you cached that Wells-Fargo money, you'd have been stiff as a poker long ago."

"Well, I got to admit you played the part of the big hero, bub. Real nice of you it was. A real Sir Gallyhad, or whatever his name was."

Holt smiled coldly. "Yeh, Sir Gallyhad and the Robin Hood of the Mogollon country, Old Cass Riker, who robs from the rich to give to the poor. The poor being Old Cass himself!"

"You got me wrong, bub."

"Listen, Old Whiskers: You got those two nice young people in that house thinking you're rich old Uncle Cass come home to give them an early Christmas. Supposing you do give them some of that money and give them all the things you promised them, and then they find out where you got the *dinero*? What then?"

The old man's eyes were as cold as glacier ice. "Now you didn't open that big month of yours and tell 'em anything about where the money come from, did you, bub? 'Cause if you did, I'll . . .''

Holt waved his Colt back and forth a little. "You'll *what*?" he asked.

"Well, you got the edge now, but I know you ain't the type to work over an old man like me to take out your spite. Look, I ain't lyin' about that money, bub. You'll get your ten thousand quick as I find out that those rattlesnakes followin' me ain't wise to where I got it hid."

Holt nodded. He let down the hammer of his Colt to half-cock, and slid the weapon into its holster. "Fair enough. How soon do we start?"

"Couple of days."

Holt smiled and shook his head. "Tomorrow."

"Now, bub!"

"Tomorrow, Old Whiskers! And just to make sure you don't get any ideas to the contrary you can bunk with me tonight, though I'd rather bunk with an old billy goat."

"Well, you ain't no rose."

Riker took his horse to the corral and

unsaddled it while Holt leaned against the fence smoking. The old coot could sure weave a mess of lies but this time Holt had him cold.

They walked back to the house and eased into it. When they were in the room, Holt jerked a thumb at the far side of the big bed, then watched Riker peel to his long johns and hop into the bed.

Holt pulled off boots and gunbelt, scaled his hat at a wall peg, then took his Colt from its sheath. "I don't sleep well, Old Whiskers," he said. "I'm nervous as hell. One time I come up out of a sound sleep and planted a bullet right through the skull of my partner's pack mule."

"Remarkable," said Cass dryly.

"Come to think of it, that danged mule looked a lot like you, but he had a little edge as to looks."

"Stop, you're killing me, bub."

Holt rolled a cigarette and lighted it. "Maybe I will one of these days, Old Whiskers, maybe I will . . ."

It was a quiet and taciturn Holt who sat

at breakfast the morning after the old buzzard had returned to the ranch. Riker could play a part with ease. He was as slick as varnish, and he had those two young people a little dewy-eyed with his conversation. Yet it seemed to Holt that every now and then he caught a feeling of tenseness, and a little tinge of fear in Riker's eyes.

"Sure, sure," the old man was saying. "Holt here and me is old *compadres*. I knew he'd be coming through this way."

"How come the two of you didn't travel together to get here," asked Tim. "Uncle Cass leave you somewhere, Holt?"

"Yes," said Holt, "he left me somewhere all right."

Cass Riker stood up and looked at Holt. "Maybe you'd like to come along?"

"Maybe I would."

"I'll get the horses."

"Do that," said Holt politely.

"I'll give you a hand, Uncle Cass," said Tim quickly.

"Sure, sure, boy, glad to have you!"

Susan leaned over and refilled Holt's

coffee cup after they left. "What were the two of you talking about last night in front of the house?"

"Odds and ends. I didn't know we had an audience."

"Do you always talk with your old *compadre* with a pistol in your hand?"

Holt felt for the makings, took them out, then looked at Susan. She nodded. He rolled a smoke and lighted it.

"You didn't answer me, Holt."

"There isn't anything for me to tell you."

"You're lying!"

"Maybe I am. There are some things that don't concern you, Susan."

"Uncle Cass does."

He eyed her. "I didn't know you loved him that much."

"It isn't him, Holt. It's Tim I'm concerned about. He has no father and no mother and I've had to fill in for both of them. We were happy enough until Uncle Cass came along. Now he's filled that boy up with big ideas, talking about money, gifts, the whole world to be placed at his feet."

"So? I don't see anything wrong with that."

"With dirty money, Holt?"

He flushed. "What do you mean by that?"

She leaned closer to him. "I'm not such a fool as you might think, Holt. Your stories don't quite hang together. He shows up here after fifteen years looking like a saddle tramp, talking about money, money until I wondered if he was in his right mind. Then he vanishes to somewhere, never saying where he was going, and then *you* show up, on the run from the law, practically cut to ribbons.

"I almost believed that story of yours that you had nothing to do with those killings on the Colorado."

He stood up and snubbed out his cigarette. "You still believe me," he said.

"Why do you say that?"

"You wouldn't have covered up for me yesterday if you hadn't believed me."

She looked away. "I want to believe you," she said.

"Well, in any case, I'll be out of your way before too long."

"On the run again?"

He looked down at her. "What difference does it make?"

"It might make a difference to me, Holt."

Then an impulse made him bend down, lift her chin with his hand, and kiss her on the lips. She did not resist. He walked to the door and looked back at her. "Forget about me, Susan," he said. "I'm nothing but a lone rider. Here today and gone tomorrow."

"Caring little about yourself and less about other people, is that it?"

"I suppose so. I don't like it any better than you do, Susan."

She stood up and began to clear the table. "Tim thinks a lot of you, Holt."

"I'm glad to hear that."

She studied him. "Don't let him down, Holt. Whatever Uncle Cass has done, and wherever he got the money might hurt

Tim for the rest of his life. I don't want to know. But you know, and somehow I believe that you'll work this thing out so that Tim doesn't get hurt."

"And you?"

She turned away. "When you said you were leaving that was hurt enough."

"Holt!" called Cass from the corral.

"Coming!"

He walked back to Susan and took her in his arms. He kissed her gently and she lightly touched the livid scar on his face, then kissed him in return, placing her head against his chest when she took her lips from his. He held her close, then released her and walked to the door. There was nothing he could say although his mind was confused and filled with teeming thoughts. She knew Cass Riker had not made his fortune in Mexico, or anywhere else. But with a deep feminine intuition she had seemed to cast aside Holt Deaver's faults and had called upon him to show his virtues.

He walked to the corral and swung up onto his horse.

Cass pulled down his disreputable hat. "You might need your rifle, Holt," she said casually. "Might run into a deer or two, and I'm partial to fresh venison."

"I'll get it!" said Tim. He ran toward the house.

Riker fiddled with his right stirrup. "Well?" he asked.

"She's on to you, Cass."

"I'm beginning to think so."

"So?"

The old man shrugged. "I earned that money. Fifteen years it cost me."

"And you're going to give most of it to them, is that it?" said Holt sarcastically. "You make me sick! You *ever* tell the truth?"

"Maybe I am this time."

Holt grunted. "I'll believe it when I see it."

"Stick around."

Holt swiveled his eyes and held the old man's attention. "I aim to do just that, Old Whiskers."

Tim came from the house and handed

Holt the rifle. "*Gracias*," said Holt as he slid the Winchester into its sheath.

They kneed their horses away from the boy and rode down the canyon. Susan Morris came out on the front porch and watched them as they rode. Holt glanced back. He seemed still to taste the soft freshness of her lips and her words came back to him. *When you said you were leaving that was hurt enough.*

"Nice girl that," said Cass.

"For once you're telling the truth."

"I don't want nothin' to happen to her, Holt."

"Meaning?"

The hard old eyes flicked at Holt. "You know what I mean, bub. You'll get your money. I promise you that. But that's *all* you'll take away from the Bandera country. Understand?"

Holt looked away from the old man. He knew Cass meant what he said. Maybe the old man *did* have a virtue or two left although it was almost impossible to believe.

Holt looked back at the house. She was gone.

"You know where we're heading?" asked Riker.

"For the *dinero*?"

"Not yet."

Holt eyed him.

"I want to take a look at those boys on the West Fork."

"Fair enough, but no killing, Riker."

They rode downstream until they rounded a huge shoulder of rock, which cut off the view of the ranch buildings. Cass turned his horse and began to ride up a long slanting fault in the canyon wall, hardly wide enough for a horse. He glanced back. "We can come out on the West Fork about half a mile from where they are by going this way."

"A real highway, ain't it?"

"If you're scared, bub, you can go back. This is *man's* work."

Holt only grunted. The old man had more than his share of guts. You had to give him credit for that at least. Holt couldn't help but wonder what it had

been like in the old days to ride behind
Cass Riker. The old coot would have to
show a little more guts if they ever ran
face on into the boys on the West Fork
of the Bandera. He had been running at
Alamo Springs, and he had run from
Verde. Maybe he aimed to run again and
leave Holt Deaver to face their enemies.
Well, he could try, but Holt was going to
stick to him like a cockleburr on a saddle-
blanket, and never give him another
chance.

9

THE early afternoon sun slanted down into the canyon of the Bandera and glinted from the swiftly running waters of the stream. The wind swayed the trees and made them form dappled patches of shade on the clear waters. The two men lay belly flat on a ridge overlooking most of the canyon, watching the simple camp far below them. Cass Riker handed the field glasses to Holt. "I can see only one of them down there. It's Pete Shalen I think. Got his left arm in a sling. Maybe it's a memento of the Verde."

Holt focused the glasses and studied the camp. There was only one man there as Cass had said. A horse and a mule grazed not far away. And there was no sign of any of the others. "I wonder where they are?" he said.

Cass rested his bearded chin on his

crossed forearms. "That's a good question. Looking for you, I guess."

"Only two of them are interested in me. But all five of them are interested in *you*."

"How so?"

Holt told him of how Morg Mills and Trump Foster had thrown in with the others back on the Verde. "Between me and you, Old Whiskers, if those five buzzards ever get their hands on that money, won't any of them sleep easy as long as they're in each other's company."

Cass grunted deep in his throat. "Gives me an idea," he said with a queer glint in his hard eyes. "Why not let 'em get their hands on the money? Then after two or three of 'em get killed off by their *compadres*, we can move in on the survivors and wipe them out? We get rid of them and we get the money."

"You sure think big!"

The old man grinned. "You have to admit it's not a bad idea."

Holt raised the field glasses again. He wasn't as much worried about the outlaws as he was about the law being after him. "What about Wells-Fargo?" asked Holt. "Don't you think they might be interested in where you hid that loot?"

"I suppose so. I never saw any of their agents waiting around Yuma for me. 'Course, I was in one helluva big rush to get outa there before those three ex-*compadres* of mine threw a loop on me."

"That figures. One thing bothers me though. Supposing Wells-Fargo agents come to the ranch looking for you? Or our five friends go there. What happens then?"

Cass grinned. "Wells-Fargo don't know about them two kids and neither does my three ex-*compadres*."

"Sure, sure, but you came back and shot off your mouth to them about all that money. Supposing they talk about it?"

"Who's going to find out where the money come from?"

"You dumb-block! They'll find you some day, won't they?"

Cass Riker spat. "No," he said quietly.

"They won't ever find me, Holt, 'cause I ain't goin' to be around."

Holt lowered the glasses and looked at him. "You mean you're going to give them the money and then pull out?"

"You figure right, bub."

"What makes you think they'll want that kind of money?"

"A blasted fortune in their hands and they're goin' to ask where it comes from?"

"Maybe they will," said Holt quietly. "Maybe they won't want it."

The old man stared at him. "Maybe you're loco," he said.

"Look, Old Whiskers! Maybe some people don't figure the way you do. Maybe some people are honest. 'Course, how would *you* know? You ain't been around anyone that's honest for so long you wouldn't know one if you saw one."

"I know you, bub," said Cass coldly.

"What I said still goes. Don't judge other people by me, Old Whiskers." Holt looked down on the camp again. "It wouldn't surprise me none if your niece and nephew didn't turn that money in to Wells-Fargo."

"Who's going to tell 'em it's Wells-Fargo money? You?"

"I ain't crazy. They'll find out by themselves likely enough. By that time I'll be in Sonora dickering for my own rancho with that ten thousand you owe me."

"Yeh," said Cass dryly.

Holt looked at him. "There's only one big thing bothering me, Cass. If any of those buzzards get to the ranch they won't go easy on those two there. They'll try to get them to talk."

"They don't know nothing about the money."

"Maybe not, but Carley and the others don't know that." Holt cased the glasses. "They sure could make it rough on them if they had a mind to."

Cass Riker wet his thin lips and looked uncertainly at Holt. "I never thought of that."

"Well, you'd better think of it!"

"Yeh . . . yeh . . . Mebbe we'd better take a look back there?"

Holt sat up and gently fingered his healing scar. "We were going after the money, Old Whiskers. Maybe I ain't changed my mind about that."

Cass stood up and began to scratch his lean stomach and when he took his hand away it held a double-barreled derringer in it, and the little gun with the big bite was pointed right at Holt's belly. "I don't know about you, Deaver," said the old man, "but I'm going back to the ranch."

Holt looked down at the gun and then into the hard eyes of the old man. "Your argument is most convincing, Old Whiskers," he said dryly. "Maybe I'd better go along with you."

"Ahead of me, *amigo*. Ahead of me!"

Holt shrugged. He led the way to the horses. They mounted and rode back toward the dangerous trail by which they had approached the West Fork of the Bandera, and this time the young man was in the lead.

They had left the horses behind the huge shoulder of rock that jutted out into the canyon, and had made their way on foot through the thick brush and trees that bordered the west side of the canyon until the ranch was in view. A scarf of smoke drifted up from the chimney but there was no sign of life about the place.

The two of them squatted down in the brush and studied the house. "Looks peaceful enough," said Cass. There was a worried note in his voice.

Holt nodded. He uncased the field glasses and focused them, sighting them on the house. There were no strange horses around the place. There were two horses in the corral and one of them was Tim's sprightly little mare, while the other was an old timer, practically retired, that used to haul the doctor's buggy in the days when he had had his practice.

"What do you think?" asked the old man.

Holt shrugged. "I know one thing: I'm not going to ride up to that house as a prime target for someone."

"Ain't no one there other than the kids," said Cass. "You can see the boy's hoss and you got Susan's hoss."

Holt nodded. "Well, let's Indian up on the place."

"We'll sure look silly if Susan and Tim see us."

"We'll look a lot sillier if those four hardcases are waiting down there for us."

"You sure are nervous, bub."

Holt spat. "You weren't exactly calm and collected this morning when you were eating breakfast."

The old man did not answer. They kept to the woods until they were up behind the ranch buildings. Still no sign of life. Cass tapped Holt on the shoulder and pointed toward the house. A fresh puff of smoke had drifted up from the chimney. "It's all right," said the old man. "Susan just fed the fire."

Holt rubbed his jaw. "You can see through those log walls, Old Whiskers?"

"I ain't ascared to go down and make sure," said Cass.

Holt shrugged. They walked down the slope to the back of the barn, looked up and down the winding stream, then walked toward the house. "Susan!" called out Cass.

"Yes, Uncle Cass!" she called from a kitchen window.

"You all right, honey?"

"Certainly, Uncle Cass!"

"See? said the old man to Holt. "You and yer ideas!"

They walked toward the back door of the house feeling a little foolish. "We can send Tim for the hosses," said Cass.

Holt nodded. He was tired, for he had not yet fully recovered his strength. Beyond that he was getting weary of the whole business. He had been living with it too long.

The kitchen door swung open and Susan stood there looking at them. Her face was a little pale. Something warned Holt. He dropped behind the old man, turned his head quickly from side to side, and as he looked toward the south wall of the house saw a lean shadow move. "Look out, Cass!" he yelled.

There was Ernie Carley standing behind Susan. The tall man shoved the girl aside and raised a six-shooter. Morg Mills came around the side of the house. "Get Deaver!" he yelled.

Holt dare not fire toward the girl. He swung and drew, facing Morgan Mills. It was then that he saw Savvy Harris framed in the barn door with a Colt in his hand. Holt whirled and fired from the hip even as Harris fired. Harris' slug whipped through the slack of Holt's shirt. The gunman staggered a little and pumped out two more shots which went wild as Holt slammed another slug into him. He went down and lay still.

Morgan Mills fired twice at Holt from the shelter of the side of the house, but Holt had hit the ground an instant before the first shot and fired from the ground a bullet which struck the log closest to Mills' face, scattering bark against it, temporarily blinding the man.

Ernie Carley dodged to one side to avoid hitting Cass and tried to get a shot in at Holt, but Susan shoved the tall man and his shot whispered past Holt's left ear.

Cass had turned and ran. He gripped the top rail of the corral and vaulted over it as cleanly as an athlete, striking the soft ground inside the corral. He dashed across the corral and over the far fence to vanish into the woods.

Holt jumped for cover inside the barn, rapping out a shot toward Morg Mills who was clutching his face. The gunman vanished from Holt's view.

Then Ernie Carley jumped back inside the house, shoving Susan ahead of him. Holt raised his pistol, and as he did so a rifle flatted off from across the creek and the slug smashed into the framing of the barn door. He dropped flat. Now he knew where Trump Foster was. Holt and Cass had been neatly suckered in by the four outlaws.

Holt crawled across the barn floor until he could peer through an unchinked place. Gun smoke still drifted about the rear of the house. There was no sign of Morg Mills or Ernie Carley. Trump Foster was not to be seen but Holt knew the big man was better than most men with the long gun and he'd have a bead on that barn door right now.

One of the five would never trouble Holt again. Savvy Harris had died as he had lived, fast and violently. It had been a near thing out there, and if it hadn't been for Susan, Holt might be lying out there beside Savvy Harris. The old man had been a big help. He had broken all records getting out of bullet range and hadn't fired a shot. Morg Mills had yelled to get Holt. They wanted him out of the way. They wanted the old man alive to find out where he had cached the loot. Now they had Susan as a hostage and quite likely they had Tim, too.

Holt opened the loading gate of his Colt and refilled the cylinder, mentally cursing himself for leaving his rifle on his horse.

"Deaver!" called Carley from inside the house.

"Yes?" answered Holt. He quickly moved his position so as not to be pinpointed.

"We don't want you, we want Riker."

"That's not what Mills said."

"Hell! You've been nothing but trouble for us. I don't know how you're still alive, but that can't be helped."

"Thanks."

Holt crawled to the far side of the barn and stood up just beyond a narrow window. He could see the back of the house and the place about where Trump Foster should be.

"We've got the woman and the boy here, Deaver! We know who they are! Now we want that old sidewinder to come along peaceful like. We got some talking to do."

"You saw him take off, Carley."

"Yes. But it's up to you to get him back."

"Why me?"

There was a few minutes of silence and then Morg Mills spoke from somewhere inside the house. "You want these people to get killed, Deaver?" he said in his cold, toneless voice.

The man meant it. He was as cold-gutted as a shark. They had all the aces. Trouble was Holt had little faith in Cass

Riker, and he wasn't at all sure the old coot would come back peaceful like as Carley would want him to.

"You hear me, Deaver?" called Morg Mills.

"Go ahead and kill them," said Holt on a long shot.

It was quiet again for a time, then Mills called out again. "I know you better than that, Deaver. You always had a soft spot in your head for other people. That's why you didn't pitch in with me and the boys back at the Colorado."

Holt knew then that Susan Morris would know that he had spoken the truth. Susan didn't know men like Morg Mills and Trump Foster.

Mills laughed. "Trouble for you is that the story is out that you were in on the deal, Deaver. Fact is, no one seems to know the names or descriptions of any of the others mixed up in it."

I do . . . thought Holt.

"Now, Deaver," said Carley clearly, "you just go and get that old goat and bring him back. We want him delivered or these two people here will die. That's clear enough. As for you, you can beat it. Webb Harris died of a busted neck and it was Savvy who wanted to make you pay for it, not me and Pete. Well, you got Savvy too. That's one less for the big payoff."

"What about Morg Mills? It was his brother I killed. Morg won't ever forget that!"

Again a long silence although Holt could have sworn he heard low voices in the house.

"Deaver?" It was Morg Mills.

"Shoot!"

"Mike is gone. Ain't no use in digging up the dead. I got to look out for myself from now on. You bring in Riker and I'll forget you killed Mike."

"All right! What's the deal?"

There might be time for Holt to get into town and bring out the sheriff and some of his boys.

Carley spoke up. "You pull out after we leave. You won't shoot, for we'll have the woman and the boy with us. You get

140

the old man and bring him to Slide Rock on the West Fork of the Bandera."

"Where will you be?"

Carley laughed. "Wouldn't you like to know? You figure we don't know you're thinking of bringing down the law?"

Holt crawled to the other side of the barn to spot Trump Foster. He saw a horse toss its head amongst the trees of a basket across the river, and the sun glinted on something else—the barrel of a rifle.

"When you get to Slide Rock we'll let you know what to do, Deaver."

They'd let him know all right, with a bullet through the back. But there was nothing else he could do, not now, in any case. He had to play their game and wait for a break. He knew well enough that once they got their hands on Riker and made him talk neither Riker or his kind would ever be found again. They'd get Holt too if they had a chance.

"Agreed, Deaver?" called out Carley.

"All right. How much time do I have?"

"Twenty-four hours."

"Give me a break, Carley!"

"He said twenty-four hours," said Morg Mills in his flat voice. "You have Riker at Slide Rock in twenty-four hours. You have him there by three o'clock tomorrow afternoon. That's final."

There was nothing for him to do but watch them take Susan and Tim as living shields until they reached the bridge and vanished into the woods.

Holt wiped the cold sweat from his face. He walked outside and rolled a cigarette, then remembered Trump Foster, and jumped back behind the house.

The wind ruffled the bloodstained shirt of Savvy Harris. "The least they could have done was to bury their own carrion," said Holt.

He dragged the body to a hollow several hundred yards from the house, rolled it in a ragged tarpaulin, then covered the body with boards, and piled rocks atop that. It would do until a better burial could be arranged.

He rolled a smoke and walked downstream until he reached the place where

142

he and Cass had left the horses. The horse Holt had been riding was still there, grazing peacefully. But there was no sign of the horse Cass Riker had ridden.

Holt rode slowly back to the ranch. He tried to figure out where the old man might have gone. He drew rein behind the house and looked up at the west canyon wall, already deep in shadow as the sun sank. He wouldn't have gone west into Tonto country. That left north, east and south. Maybe he had gone south to get his money.

10

IT was dusk when he headed away from the ranch. He had done a little hard and fast thinking too, trying to fit the odd-shaped pieces of the jigsaw puzzle together. Susan had told him that Uncle Cass had gone south for a week or ten day's journey, yet it had been less than a week when he had showed up at the ranch. Then, by great fortune, he had spotted the outlaws on the West Fork of the Bandera when he was on his way back with the money. He said he had cached it for fear that they might see him and capture him. Therefore the money at least was on the West Fork. And if Holt Deaver knew Old Whiskers as he thought he did, the old coot would have headed for the West Fork as well as the others.

It would be real cosy there. The four hardcases, Susan and Tim, Cass Riker, thousands of dollars in stolen money, and

Holt Deaver, riding into trouble with a ranch girl's apron as his guerdon. Meanwhile, somewhere out in the blue might be Burl Stuart, US Marshal and Deputy-Sheriff Lang Masters, all with a special interest in him.

With only twenty-one hours left in which to deliver Cass Riker, Holt Deaver drew rein at the foot of the insanely dangerous trail. It wasn't in the cards for Holt Deaver to die from a fall. The Fates had other plans, not quite ready as yet, but probably just as violent and just as final. Thinking this, he ascended the treacherous slope.

The moon had not yet risen when he reached the ridge that overlooked the West Fork of the Bandera and the camp they had spotted earlier in the day.

He led the horse quietly down the ridge and along the canyon floor, half expecting a hoarse challenge out of the night. Would they fire upon him? They expected him to find Cass Riker, so perhaps they would be content to let the full twenty-four hours pass; *but they knew he was there now.*

He found the place where the camp had been. The ground was still warm from the fire. Slide Rock was further upstream; Cass Riker had mentioned it earlier that day. The whole area in that stretch of the canyon was known as Slide Rock, but the huge mass of detritus that formed the wide talus slope and gave the area its name was not in sight from the camp area.

Holt felt a touch of panic creep up in his mind. So little time! He followed the stream toward the slide area. A thought came to him. Cass had said he had *seen* the outlaws camp, then had cached the loot for the second time, so the place where he had seen the camp could not be too far. Holt stopped at a point where the canyon trended northeast, then looked back. Dark as it was he knew that no one could see the camp once he passed around the canyon bend. But if a man was up high he might be able to see *over* it.

The rock formations of the area were

deteriorating, and many places had decayed. It was outright insanity to try and scale those walls even in daylight. The moon would be up before long to give him plenty of light, but he couldn't wait. If he only knew that country better!

He led the horse into a box canyon and picketed it near a pool of water, took his Winchester, some food, his reata, then he formed a rifle sling from several saddle straps and slung the weapon on his back.

There was a faint suggestion of moonlight to the east when he started his climb. It was easy enough until he reached the first naked shoulder of rock. By the time he was halfway up the canyon wall, great shards hung by the weakest of joints to the massive rock.

He scouted gingerly along the base of the decomposed rock formations, thrusting a hand into catclaw now and then, and feeling the stinging whip of cholla through the thin material of his levis. The moon was making a silvered path of the West Fork of the Bandera when he found a place that looked less risky than any other place. There was no other choice.

Feeling his way step by step, he dared not look down. The sweat ran down his gaunt body and stung his freshly-healing cuts. His temples throbbed and his guts became queasy. He knew he might never make it.

Then he felt a little surge of triumph, for he could see the lip of the canyon about twenty feet above him. He reached for a hold and got a firm grip when suddenly his footing sank beneath him, and with a roaring, rushing and grating of tons of rock the whole formation let go to pour in a dusty mass down to the canyon below. As he hung there, fighting with fingertips and toes for claw holds, he heard the last pitiful whinnying of his horse as it was crushed and buried beneath the rock.

He was unable to go up or down, and the racing seconds of doom pattered through his mind like the final pattering of bits and shards on the slope.

With his leg and arm muscles tiring,

Holt cautiously felt along the thin line of a rock ledge above him until his strong fingers felt a groove. He thrust out his right foot and tapped with it along the rock until it found a hold. After breathing a short prayer, he swung himself until he could grip the groove with both hands and let his full weight depend on them until his boot toes scrabbled into holds.

Then inch by inch he worked up the rock face; it seemed as though that twenty feet were more like twenty miles. Suddenly the strange and horrible delusion came over him that the rock was leaning out toward him and that he was scaling further and further back, until it seemed he would be hanging there in space.

Staring at the rock inches from his nose, he worked slowly and steadily upward until at last his questing right hand struck the top. He paused, then exerted the last of his strength, swung his whole body upward and rolled away from that damnable edge.

The surface of the rocky ground

seemed to float and heave beneath him and his hands remained clawed and tense as he lay there fighting nausea and panic. It was a long time until he could raise his head, then his body, to look about him.

The moon was flooding the country with light now, lending a cold-looking and eerie pattern to the rock formations and stunted trees, making it into an imitation of a lunar landscape; he had the odd impression that perhaps he had climbed from the earth into some alien land.

There was nothing to be gained by sitting there. He rose and rolled a cigarette, studying the terrain until the cigarette was finished. Then he walked off with long easy strides to the north. Now and then he walked almost to the edge of the canyon brink and peered down, but there was no place that looked any easier than the place he had scaled. Now, if he had climbed to a place where there was no trail in or out, he'd have to descend the canyon wall—and that could be more dangerous than climbing it. He shuddered a little as he thought of the tons and tons of rock that had broken loose back there to almost bury the horse.

He glanced ahead and to his right. The wide shelf had narrowed somewhat and had curved to follow the rock face to his right with still no indication of opening or passage through the brooding wall of rock. But the formation had changed to a rather odd-looking conglomeration of geometrically patterned rock, much darker than the rest of the rock facing. It was a curious sort of a country, with continual surprises for a man, but this beat all.

Staring at the formation with squinted eyes, he walked on, and then suddenly he stopped and opened his eyes widely. "By God," he said hoarsely, "that ain't rock! It's buildings!"

He reached back for his Winchester and pulled it forward to lever a round into the chamber. He let the hammer down to halfcock then paced forward slowly and softly with his head turning from side to side to scan each foot of ground. He was within two hundred yards of them when he realized what they were. Someone, probably years ago, had built those buildings about a mine. But how had they managed to get in there to bring in building materials and mining machinery and how did they get the ore out of there? It was an unanswered question but he did know one thing for sure; there was a way in and out of that dangerous rock shelf, and he aimed to find it.

When he was closer he noticed the red scaling rust on the metal structures and the silvery-gray of the unpainted, warped wood. Shreds of tattered canvas waved back and forth in the wind and somewhere within the group of buildings a door suddenly banged, slammed shut by the invisible hand of the wind. The ruins were imposing even against the great backdrop of the rock wall towering behind them. The shaky metal and wood scaffolding etched angles and triangles against the lighter-colored rock. It had been a Paul Bunyan feat to bring in material to construct such buildings and other structures. But the men who had built the place and had worked it had left long ago and now it was the haunt of bats, mice, rattlesnakes and utter loneliness.

But it was no time to admire the guts of the men who had built such a place in the almost inaccessible canyon of the West Fork of the Bandera in a hard search for fortune. Holt Deaver was looking for a man who had found, or rather appropriated, a fortune not by sweating blood in a hellhole of a canyon, but by cashing in his six-shooters at Wells-Fargo. Time was running as swiftly as it always did when a big game was in progress and the chips were down.

Holt wiped the sweat from his face and grounded his rifle. He looked to his left, along the great rock shelf and saw that wheels and hoofs of bygone days had etched a roadway there. So there was a way out and it was plain enough to see, but somehow or another he could not drag himself away from the great rusty and decaying ghost town that squatted on the rock before him.

He walked between two buildings and halted to eye the sort of street that ran from left to right in front of him, littered with rusted tin cans, broken bottles, pieces of rusted machinery almost impossible to identify. The buildings all had the same hangdog, forlorn look of the ghost town, almost as though furtively hoping they'd be used again, but knowing they never would.

He looked up the slope toward the mine machinery set against the face of the rock wall and it almost seemed to him there was a quick, almost unseen movement in the darkness of the base structure. He wet his lips and raised his rifle. He waited and watched with the spidery patience he had learned in his scouting days. Then, as so often happened, his eyes began to play their little tricks engendered by the shifting moonlight, the movements of canvas, tin or wood actuated by the wind.

He tried an old trick. He closed his eyes, waited, then quickly opened them and this time he was sure he saw something move. A whitish, grayish sort of substance, moved by the wind.

Holt eased back, passed behind the building, avoided walking on a rusted sheet of metal, then walked between the next two buildings, taking off his hat as he did so. He got down on his knees and peered around the side of the building, knowing he was in thick shadow. This time he could see the base structure from a different angle. Once again he closed and opened his eyes and again he saw the fluttering object.

He moved back once more. He wasn't sure what it was but his instinct probed him to take a closer look.

He was within fifty yards of the base structure, close by the low wall of a vat, flat on his lean belly, when he saw the movement again. *I'll be double-damned*, he thought, *it ain't possible!*

Holt inched backward, then crawled around the base of the vat until he could again peer at the structure. This time he was sure. He faded into the shadows near the base of the rock wall, then padded forward. His silence seemed impossible for a man of his size, but he went as softly as the night-hunting owl he had seen a little while back.

He was within twenty feet of the object when it moved slowly, fluttering in the wind. He froze, then as the object moved into the thicker shadows he cat-footed forward like a puma. Just as the object turned and looked at him, his rifle muzzle moved out and rested comfortably on a lean gut and the hammer was thumbed back to full cock. "Hello, Old Whiskers," said Holt coldly. "I might of knowed this would be a good place for you to hole up in."

The grayish-white whiskers thrust out toward Holt and moved pugnaciously in the wind. "Why?" asked Cass Riker sourly.

Holt jerked his head. "The bat, the rat, the snake and the hootie owl like these places, and by godfrey, Old Whiskers, I do believe you found yourself a real home with your furred and feathered kin."

"Gawddamn you, boy, take that rifle muzzle outa my navel!"

Holt grinned evilly. "You old snake. Why'd you run off like that?"

Cass Riker looked away. "Well, I didn't see no sense in standing there like a damned ol' wooden Indian to get shot full of lead."

"It was all right for *me* to stand there though, wasn't it?"

"Well, you got to allow you ain't too bright, bub." The bright old eyes glittered in the cold moonlight. "You got more luck than brains, I gotta admit. They hit you at all?"

"No."

"Well, we can't expect *everything*. You get any of them?"

"One."

"Only *one*? Boy, you oughta stay outa gun scrapes, if that's the best you can do," jeered Cass. "Who'd you do in?"

"Savvy Harris."

Riker paled a little. "That was him in the barn, weren't it, bub?"

"It were, bub."

The old man nodded. He rubbed his whiskery jaw. "He fired first though?"

Holt nodded.

"That's what I thought. By godfrey I woulda never believed it, bub. You know something?"

"No."

"You're damned near as fast as me. Now I . . ."

Holt leaned on the rifle a little. "Shut up," he said. "We've talked long enough. We're going to take a little trip, Cass."

"Where to?" asked the old man suspiciously.

"Down to Slide Rock."

Riker laughed. "You loco, bub? I know them boys are down there somewheres. I didn't see 'em but I heard 'em. They got a gal with 'em too. Probably figurin' on a real blowout down there. Likker and a woman. Might be interestin' to go at that. Haww!" His face changed. "Where'd they get a filly in this damned country?"

"Don't you know, Cass?" asked Holt softly.

The hard eyes narrowed. "God's sake! I never thought of that!"

"They got the boy too, Cass."

Riker paled. "You let 'em? I oughta . . ."

"You oughta what?" jeered Holt. "Old Footloose, you left there fast and furious like the devil beating tanbark! Now keep that waggin' jaw still while I tell you the story."

Riker listened quietly while Holt told him of the deal he had been forced to make. "They mean it too, Cass," said Holt. "They'd kill those two like a man drowns unwanted kittens, if you don't show up and pay off."

Riker shook his head as though to clear it. "You know what will happen to me, and maybe them anyways if I pay off?"

Holt nodded. "And we can't go to the law."

"Hell no! You plumb loco to think that? We'd lose the whole damned kit and caboodle, lock, stock and barrel!"

"Meaning the money?"

The wind sighed softly through the

ironwork of the structure over them and what it sighed about sent a cold chill through Holt Deaver and he wondered suspiciously if Cass Riker felt the same way.

"Well," said Cass, "we can't stand here like two crows on an outhouse roof, least-ways, not with a rifle in my belly." He placed a hand on the barrel and tried to move it away but it was as rigid as a girder. "How come?" demanded Riker.

"This may strike you as a bellybuster, Old Whiskers, but I don't exactly trust you."

"Sho, bub, but we got to work *together* now to figger a plan."

Holt stepped back and let the hammer down to half cock. "Walk," he said quietly. "*Ahead* of me."

They walked down to one of the buildings and sat down on the porch. Holt rolled a smoke and passed the makings to Riker. They lighted up and sat there silently for a time.

"Three o'clock you said?" asked Riker at last.

"Yes. I hope to God you got your cache not too far from here."

"I ain't sayin' *where* it is!"

Holt tapped the knuckles of his right hand with the fingertips of his left hand. "You will, bub, *you will*."

Riker held his head in his gnarled hands. "I just can't think of a way outa this, Holt."

"We have no choice."

The wind soughed through the great canyon and whispered dryly around the buildings and mine structures. Holt leaned back against a post and suddenly a thought came to him. The old man had been hiding there. Damned if he wouldn't have the loot there too! Holt was slow on the brain, quick on the trigger.

Riker sighed, flipped away his cigarette, then reached for the makings. "All right," he said quietly. "The cache is here at the mine. Slide Rock ain't no more than three miles from here. We got plenty time to make that. All we need is time to think of a plan." He rolled a second smoke and lighted it and his hard little eyes studied Holt over the flare of the match. "We got some advantages and they got others. We got the money and they got the kids. Now all we have to do is to get the money to them four buzzards and get them two lambs outa their hands, without them gettin' killed."

"And us," said Holt.

Riker spat to one side. "I ain't thinkin' about myself no more, Holt."

He sounded so utterly sincere that Holt *almost* believed him.

11

THEY sat there as the moon waned, slowly eating the food brought from the ranch by Holt, sipping at the water, and not looking at each other. No inspiration had come to them, and yet they knew right well that in a matter of some hours they would have to have some solution.

Holt finished his meal and then rolled a cigarette. "There's one thing we can do, Cass," he said thoughtfully. "They told me to bring you to Slide Rock, but they didn't say anything about bringing the money there too."

"Figgered you might be tempted," said Riker slyly.

Holt ignored him. "They said I should bring you there, but I won't go."

"Meaning?"

Holt sucked in on his cigarette and

blew a smoke ring. "Maybe they expect me too, but I won't get there."

Riker eyed him suspiciously. "They might not like that. They might raise hell, Holt."

"Let them! What do they really want? Me or you? Hell no! They want that money. When they seen you they figure you'll have to lead them to the money, and they'll damned quick forget about me."

"That don't make sense when I tell them you found me."

Holt spat. "How you ever engineered that Wells-Fargo deal is beyond me. Dumb luck I call it. You don't tell them I found you! You just say you saw them with the two prisoners and figured they were using them as hostages, and you, being the kindly old Uncle Cass, come in to give yourself up."

"They won't buy that bill of goods!"

Holt nodded slowly. "Yes they will, because I'm going to be dead, Old Whiskers."

"I'm for it, bub, but ain't that the *hard* way to do it?"

Holt looked up at the sky in silent prayer, as though asking for strength to go on. "I won't be dead! I'll be where the loot is cached, and I'll make my play when you bring them here for it. It will be touch and go and the devil will get the hindmost, but I can't think of any other way out."

"You think they'll believe you're dead?"

Holt smiled indulgently. "You poor old man. I got to tell you everything? We're going to make it *look* as though I died. You remember hearing a helluva rock fall some hours before I got here?"

"Yes."

"I made that rock slide! I swear, Cass, it sounded as though the whole canyon wall fell in, and my hoss is down there, with his legs sticking up out of the fallen rock. Now you're going to go to that slide pile and plant enough stuff around that hoss to make it look as though I was caught under it too."

"You think they'll buy that pig in a poke?"

Rolling a smoke for himself, Holt grinned. "Look, Old Whiskers, whether they buy that pig in a poke or not, it's the only plan we got."

Holt walked softly through the ruins until he managed to kill a large rat with a blow from his Winchester butt. He stripped off his hat band and ripped off a shirt sleeve, tore at the hat and crushed it, and then opened the rat with his sheath knife and dabbled the blood on the articles. He carried the things to Cass Riker who sniffed suspiciously.

"We have until three o'clock tomorrow afternoon," said Holt. "You'd better get out of here before daylight and get to the fallen rock before the dawn. Plant the stuff, then get out of there and go the long way around before you reach Slide Rock. Get there around noon. Now, you make it look like you just happened to see them with their prisoners and came in by yourself."

"Supposing they split up? Leave the

kids somewheres with a guard whilst I bring the others up here for the *dinero*? That would fox *us*, bub."

Holt shrugged. "It's another risk. Between thee and me, Old Whiskers I think the four of them will stay together. There ain't no honor amongst thieves, like the book says."

Riker squinted a little as he studied Holt. "Yeh, I been thinking about that."

"Well look at someone else then."

They discussed their plan for another half-hour. It would be touch and go and the lead would fly and maybe the two of them might not make it; maybe the young woman and the boy might not make it either. But there was nothing else to do unless they stalked the four outlaws and their captives, trying to pick them off one by one; but the risks in such an action would be greater than what they had planned.

Holt looked at the dying moon. "One more thing to do, Cass."

"So?"

"Show me where the loot is."

There was a tense silence from the old man.

"Well?"

Riker tugged at his beard, spat leisurely, squinted at the sky, then at the ground.

"Riker!"

Cass stood up. "How will I know whether you'll be here or not when I bring 'em back?"

"Meaning?"

"All that money left here with a broke saddle bum whilst Old Whiskers trots down into the canyon and gives hisself up to them sidewinders? What proof do I have that you'll be here?"

"My word."

They stood there eyeing each other. Then Holt reached inside his shirt and took out Susan's apron. He silently handed it to Riker.

Riker fingered the material, then looked at Holt.

"I get the message, Holt. You win. Let's go."

Holt followed the old man toward the

mining structure over the mine itself. It was getting darker now with the death of the moon and a colder wind sighed through the canyon. Holt shivered a little.

Riker walked like a cat through the litter and beneath the lower part of the structure. He felt about, then Holt heard the creaking of hinges and felt a draft of cool, earthy-smelling air flow about him.

"Here," said Cass. "Strike a light."

He handed Holt a candle lantern. Holt lighted it and held it up. The guttering, yellow light revealed a thick door that had been set neatly into the chiseled rock of the mine entrance.

Holt leaned the rifle against the side of the mine entrance and then followed Cass. He held the lantern up high as they walked. The old man was right. The going was rough. Rock had fallen as well as a pit prop; rusting machinery, balks of wood and abandoned gear littered the narrow passageway. On and on they went into the echoing darkness until Cass turned sharply right into a drift and walked steadily onward. The drift was narrower and just as cluttered. A cold draft poured about them.

Then Cass Riker stopped, rested a hand against a sagging prop and simply said, "Here, bub."

Holt held the lantern up higher. A number of leathern hats with brass fittings, now green with verdigris, lay on the floor of the drift.

"Take a look," said Cass quietly. "You never did believe me, did you?"

Holt hooked the lantern to a rusted spike, wiped his sweating hands on his thin levis, and went down on one knee beside the first sack. He struggled a little with the leather straps thickened with dampness and age, until at last he raised the flap and thrust in a questing hand. It struck something thick and wadded. He withdrew it and stared at a wad of bills, neatly bound with paper and elastic bands. The top bill was a one hundred dollar bill. Holt riffled through the wad. They were *all* one hundred dollar bills. The real sugar!

"There's eighty thousand eagles in

them dirty old bags, bub. When we settle this business, you get ten of them like I agreed," said Cass. His voice seemed further away, for Holt was in a vague, almost dreamlike state.

"Go ahead, bub! Count 'em!"

But just then he remembered something. Cass had said he had made a haul of eighty thousand. The saloonkeeper in Yardigan had said it had been one hundred thousand, and Morg Mills, in the conversation that Holt had overheard at the Verde, had claimed it had been one hundred and twenty thousand!

After counting the eighty thousand, he spoke over his shoulder. "This is all of it, Cass?"

There was no answer.

"You hear me, Old Whiskers?"

No answer.

He looked behind himself. There was no one there. He jumped to his feet and reached for the lantern, kicking aside several wads of the stolen money. "Cass Riker!" he called out.

"Cass Riker . . . Cass Ri . . ." The echo died tauntingly away.

Holt ran through the narrow drift, heedless of the obstructions. "Damn you, Cass!" he yelled.

He hurled himself down the main tunnel toward the doorway and just in time he saw it close and heard the rattling of metal against metal. He slammed a shoulder into the massive door and winced with cruel pain. "Riker!" he yelled hoarsely.

Then it was deathly silent except for the distant dripping of water far down the tunnel.

Holt placed the lantern on the floor and rested an ear against the damp wood of the door.

"Deaver?" came the thin faint voice of the old man.

"Damn you! Where'd you think I was?"

Riker chuckled. "Countin' that *dinero*! Was it all there, bub?"

"I'll wring your skinny neck!"

Riker laughed again, "No, you won't, 'cause you can't get outa there, bub."

"I'll smash this door down!"

"Hear him," jeered Riker. Then his voice changed and became cold and hard. "Listen, and keep that big mouth of yours shut for once! You think I was goin' to go down in that canyon and leave you up here nice and cosy with eighty thousand dollars? I ain't *that* loco."

"What's your dirty game, Riker?"

Silence again. Then Riker spoke steadily. "I'm going down there like we planned. I'm going to bring 'em up here like we planned. Only instead of finding you gone with the loot, I'll have you safe and sound in there, standing guard over it like a *patron*. You get it, bub?"

A cold feeling raised the flesh on Holt's body. The old Spanish miners used to close a mine and hide it, planning to come back some day, and as a guard they would slay one of their Indian laborers so that his ghost would guard the treasure.

Riker laughed. "You'll live! Now, when we get back here, it's up to you to take care of them. I got you spotted, bub, guarding Old Whisker's loot like a good little boy."

Holt wiped the cold sweat from his face. "Supposing you *don't* come back, Riker?"

This time there was no answer from the old man. Nothing but the dying echoes fleeing down the cold dank tunnel.

The candle was getting low, and he still had not found any way of getting out of that tomb-like mine. The main tunnel ended in a massive rock fall. It would take him days to dig through it, and even if he succeeded, he still didn't know whether it led to freedom or death. He explored drift after drift to find them ending in blank rock faces. He went back to the place where the money littered the floor of the drift and sat down on a timber to think.

What if the old coot kept on going? He'd wait until he was sure Holt was dead, then come back for the loot. Riker had outwitted three partners fifteen years ago when he had made the haul. He liked the idea of running alone through those lovely green leaves.

But Susan and Timmie were still in horrible danger down in the canyon. Maybe the old billy goat did have a sense of responsibility and maybe he planned to get rid of his pursuers alone. That would take some doing!

Hours had ticked past like the sound of a death-watch beetle. That damned door sealed the mine like the lid on a tomb and the simile was not pleasant. He rested his head in his hands and stared at his worn boot toes.

Holt idly kicked at a wad of the money. He grinned coldly. Well, the old billy goat had kept his word. Holt had his ten thousand. In fact he had *eighty* thousand, but a million times that number couldn't buy his way to freedom now.

He thought back on the days when he had worked as a miner. He had been with a blasting crew then, working under a skilled young engineer, and some of his lore had rubbed off on Holt. It was a subject he had liked, but his feet had gotten itchy and the long ride had beckoned as it usually did.

One stinking stick of dynamite might loosen that ponderous door. One stick might just make it, and he had eighty thousand dollars to pay for it. He thought back on Yardigan's and the powder house the old storekeeper kept at a safe distance behind his store.

Idly he picked up one of the decks of greasy playing cards and began to play solitaire, and as he handled the pasteboards something began to plague his mind. Something that young engineer had told him so many years ago. Something that began to work in his mind like a ferment. He slapped down the cards. Something to do with explosives! Something to do with playing cards! But what was the connection!

He reached for the bottle of liquor and pulled the cork out. The rich, fruity odor filled his nostrils. He drank deeply and felt the welcome warmth in his gut, then he played on while his mind tried to race ahead of him, to tell him something.

Then he remembered that playing cards are made of cellulose. The red ink used on the hearts and diamonds is made of glycerin and silver nitrate. A wet mass of this, tamped solidly into a pipe and capped, then heated, will form steam and gas. Glycerin and nitrate together with cellulose, under heat and compression, should form pressure enough to explode.

"Yeh," grunted Holt, "but how much of an explosion? Maybe not enough to blow my big nose."

Then he took the red cards from both sets, tearing the red spots from each card and placing them in a tin can. With a trickle of water he was able to make mush of the pasteboard. Then he searched for and found a piece of pipe capped at one end. After pouring the mess into it, he stopped the pipe up with a small piece of wood.

Anxiously, he hurried to the mouth of the tunnel. He placed the pipe upright in the angle between the wall and door, then wedged it tightly, leaving enough space to place the lantern beneath the pipe. There might just be enough heat, but it would take time, and the candle didn't have long to go. He placed heavy articles about the pipe, slid the lantern beneath it, then wedged more material into place.

He uncorked the bottle and got up on his knees to drink. The candle had almost gutted out, and his heart sank within him. He raised the bottle and took a good slug. Just as it hit his throat the blast roared along the tunnel, and a wall of gas hit him as well as a melon-sized chunk of rock.

12

IT was later than two o'clock in the afternoon by the angle of the sun when Holt Deaver finished with his preparations. He had taken the money from the drift and had re-cached it, then he had re-set the huge door, which the blast had driven forward at the bottom and off the great hinge.

The thing he wanted to do was to get Cass to lead the outlaws into the mine, hoping that they might, in their greed and excitement at the proximity of the money, just leave Susan and Timmie outside of the mine. The odds were high against that, of course, but Holt had been faced with high odds ever since he had left Chloride.

What was holding them back? He had told Cass to reach them about noon, but then you couldn't depend on the old buck. His mind worked in devious ways like the book said. Holt had no rifle, but he had his six-shooter. Six slugs against four, fast gunslingers who would have twenty-four shots from their six-guns aimed at one target.

Maybe they'd been suspicious of the old man's story about Holt Deaver being beneath that rock fall. Maybe they had dug into it. Maybe they had been suspicious of him returning alone. Morg Mills and Trump Foster didn't know the old bat too well, but Ernie Carley and Pete Shalen sure did.

The sweat of indecision ran down his body. He took a long chance and trotted to the canyon brink to look down. There was no sign of human life, but he could have sworn he saw a thin wreath of wood smoke drifting up from the trees far below. Someone was down there.

Maybe they had heard the explosion of the improvised charge Holt had devised and had become too suspicious. But the money was the lodestar. It would make them charge hell with a bucket of water.

Holt walked slowly back to the mine

keeping an eye out toward the only way up to the rock shelf. No sign of life there either. Then a cold thought raced through his head. He looked up at the ragged escarpment high above the mine. Maybe they were up there watching the mine! But there was nothing to see except a tattered fringe of pines and a lone hawk floating easily in the updraft from the deep canyon. That wary bird would have been long gone had anyone been up there.

Retreating into one of the buildings away from the warm sun, he could see the narrow shelf where the rutted road came around a rock shoulder toward the mine. Where were they? It was getting close to four o'clock by now and still no sign nor sound of them.

He risked a smoke and lay flat on his belly peering through a crack in the thin siding of the building. It was so—that a man's luck would run out. In some things at least. Some men were lucky in cards and others in love. An odd, but lingering thought entered his mind. He smashed a fist down on the warped flooring. "By godfrey," he said softly. He had almost forgotten *one* thing: The love that Susan Morris had for Holt Deaver, the lone rider! He felt inside his shirt and touched the apron, no longer crisp and fresh, but crumpled and stained with dirt and sweat.

"Susan!" he said aloud.

What was it she had said to him? *When you said you were leaving that was hurt enough*.

Then to hell with Cass Riker and his ill-gotten loot, and to hell with Ernie Carley, Pete Shalen, Morg Mills and Trump Foster! It was Susan he was fighting for now and the sudden wonder of the revelation filled him with a faith and courage he had never experienced before. He *had* to win now!

Then it was darker and darker. Somewhere off in the tangled brush of the mesa top a coyote howled mournfully.

Holt Deaver cursed. A man could hardly see his hand in front of his face now and if they came at that time it would be touch and go. It would be some hours before the full moon arose.

He paced about like a lean lobo with his hand resting on the butt of his Colt, peering into the darkness, testing the night with all his senses, straining his hearing at each sound.

Then slowly the faint light came from the east, ever so slowly, and it was then that he could distinguish objects that had vanished with the departure of the sunlight.

Yet there was nothing to warn him of their coming. No sound of hoof striking stone, or creak of saddle leather; no muted voices; no sudden whickering of a horse. Nothing . . .

At least Holt Deaver had two advantages over and above his native skills with gun, fists and boots. He had the advantage of surprise—if they believed he lay stark beneath the rock fall; he had the advantage, earned through hours of nervous wandering, of knowing the mine area like the palms of his dirty, calloused hands. Every building, structure, machine and rise or fall of ground was etched in his memory.

He raced behind a row of sagging buildings, then stopped just behind the last of them, while he raised his head and sharply drew in his breath. It had come to him at last. He had seen nothing and had heard nothing and his keen nostrils had scented nothing alien to the night, but it was there just the same!

Crouching behind a rusted pile of gears and cogs, he could watch that double ribbon of ruts worn into the soft rock. He stayed there for a long time until he saw a faint, furtive movement at the rock shoulder. He wet his dry lips with the tip of his tongue and became more conscious of the steady beating of his heart.

The movement came again. Then suddenly a man moved along the road with a rifle held in his hands, and there was no mistaking Morgan Mills, the human timber wolf. He moved as quietly as the vagrant night breeze.

Holt raised his head and looked up at the rock facing above the road. It didn't take long to spot another movement up there. A rock fell and bounced on the roadway. Trump Foster was deadly with the long gun, but he moved as softly and as cautiously as an ox. The big man went along the top of the wall, keeping pace with Mills. Holt couldn't help but grin, scared as he was. He could just imagine what Morg Mills had thought when Trump had kicked that rock over the side.

Mills reached the first of the buildings, set between the road and the rock wall, with just about enough space to make it. He peered along the line of buildings. Then he waved a hand.

A moment later two more men appeared. One of them walking ahead of the other and stumbled as he walked, for his hands were tied behind his back. There was no doubt about who he was. Just behind Riker was Ernie Carley, walking with a Colt in his right hand, while his left held a rope attached about Riker's neck in a noose which could be tightened swiftly with a pull. They

weren't taking any chances with Old
Whiskers, for the old ram could butt
viciously if he had a chance.

Then Holt felt a tightening in his throat
as he saw three more people coming
slowly up the center of the moonlit road.
Timmie was first, just ahead of his sister,
and his face was white in the moonlight.
The wind toyed with Susan's dark,
lustrous hair. She held her head high, for
there was the air of a thoroughbred about
that girl, who was now mixed in with a
pack of curs and mongrels. Holt
numbered himself amongst the last. Pete
Shalen, with his left arm still in a sling,
walked just behind the girl. She had not
been bound because she'd never be able
to outrun or dodge a slug from the pistol
he carried in his right hand.

While Trump Foster found a place to
work his way down the rock wall, Holt
lay flat. The big man joined Morgan Mills
and they walked softly past the first of
the buildings with cocked rifles swinging
steadily back and forth, covering each
door and window as they peered about.

Holt dared not move until they had passed him. He saw Susan's face clearly in the moonlight, with her lovely hazel eyes and soft mouth. Her face was set and taut as she passed. He heard the grating of their feet on the gravelly surface of the road. None of them had spoken. It had almost been like a procession of ghosts.

When next he saw them they were beneath the rusted iron structure built about the mine entrance. Then he heard the creaking of the huge door and wondered if Old Whiskers had noticed that the door didn't swing quite so easily as it had when he had closed it on Holt.

Then all of them but Trump Foster entered the mine. Foster stood in the shadows, betrayed only by the dull light of the moon on his rifle barrel. Holt inched along the shadowed side of the vat. Trump had ears and eyes like an Apache and could shoot by sound as well as by sight. A man didn't take chances with him.

There was a place beside the vat where rain water had softened the ground. It was a whitish deposit of soft earth. Holt moved his hands around in it then smeared it over his face. He cleaned his hands on his shirt, then inched along until he could stand up in the shadows of the rock wall. He freed his Colt, then walked like a cat closer and closer to Trump. If Trump turned . . . But Holt was within a few feet of him before the big man turned quickly and stared at Holt.

"Trump . . . Trump Foster," said Holt in a hollow voice.

Trump's mouth opened and his eyes widened and he seemed to freeze in position. "You're dead, Deaver," he said hoarsely.

"Come with me, Trump Foster."

"No—no."

Then Holt swung swiftly and viciously like a striking copperhead and the heavy pistol barrel caught Trump on the left temple. He swayed toward the rock face, and Holt caught the rifle from his limp hands. Trump sagged to the ground. Holt wasted not a second. He gripped the big man and dragged him roughly along the harsh ground to a place behind the cyanide vat. He had just ripped off Trump's pants belt and bandana to bind him when he heard voices in the tunnel. There was no time to pinion Trump now. He jerked the big man's holster gun free from the leather and ran like an antelope to duck in behind a building from which he could still see the mine entrance. Maybe he should have slid a knife between the man's ribs, but that wasn't Holt Deaver's way.

"Trump!" called out Morg Mills.

"Trump . . . Trump . . . Trump . . ." answered the echoes.

"He's gone," said Morg.

They all came out from beneath the rusted structure. Something black had etched itself on Cass Riker's face, something like ink, but it wasn't ink, it was blood. Riker stumbled as Ernie Carley viciously jerked the noose about the old man's neck yanking him to and fro. "Where's that loot, you damned old goat!" he snarled.

Susan reached out a hand and Morg

Mills shoved her back. Tim struck at the man, but a backhand from Mills struck the boy and drove him to the ground where he lay still.

Holt felt the hot blood rush through him. Raw courage and hate wouldn't beat those men; not yet in any case. Other weapons had to be used and Holt thought he had the answer.

Holt eased into the building beside him. He padded through it, feeling his way carefully. Then he stopped beside one of the leathern bags which he had taken from the drift. He could hear the harsh voices of the three outlaws as they lashed out at Cass Riker.

"Let him alone!" said Susan. "He doesn't know anything about money! He's never had any!"

Ernie Carley laughed. "Helluva lot you know about it! Don't let this old devil fool you. Uncle Cass! That's rich!"

"Where is the loot?" yelled Morg Mills.

"Talk, Riker, or we'll break your skinny neck," snarled Pete Shalen.

Holt peered through a window. He had

them easily in his sights. He didn't give a tinker's damn for the old man, but Susan would be in the line of fire. That group had to be split up.

Holt framed himself in the window. "You looking for money, *hombres*!" he called out. "Look!" He reached inside his shirt and took out one of the wads, snapping the band with a thumbnail, then hurled the loose bills out into the street. "Come and git it!" Morg Mills snapped a shot at him. He darted behind the building and into the next one, snatching up a wad from the pile he had left there in the middle of the floor. He broke the band and hurled the wad through the window. "Look!" he yelled. "Free *dinero* for the taking!"

Then he was gone again, running like hell past one building and into the next where he again hurled bills out into the bright moonlight. He could hear yelling and cursing, but above all the old man's voice was the clearest.

"He's gone plumb loco! Throwing my

money away like that! Plumb loco I tell you!"

He reached the last building and rounded the end of it in time to see Pete Shalen leaping up on the porch of the closest building. "Shalen," yelled Holt.

Pete had his Colt in his free hand and he snapped a shot at Holt. Holt fired twice from the hip and the second shot caught Shalen in the belly, driving him back off the porch to crash lifelessly on the moonlit ground.

Powdersmoke drifted across the street as Holt ran toward the next building. Ernie Carley was framed in the doorway. He fired twice at Holt, but Holt had hit the ground and he fired twice too, almost like an echo. One of Carley's slugs spurted dirt against Holt's face. Carley had been hit. He reeled out into the middle of the street, doing the border shift from wounded right to good left hand, but a forty-four drove upward into his chest and he fell flat on his back while his Colt skidded across the ground. Blood gushed from his mouth and flooded down onto the ground, staining it blackly.

Holt leaped to his feet and darted behind a building. "Hide, Susan!" he yelled. A shot splintered the wood near his face and he fired at the flash.

"I can't leave Tim!" she cried.

"Stay low then!"

A shot answered his command.

Then it was quiet except for the rustling of the wind. The powder smoke drifted across the street in sheets rifted by the wind. Two dead men stared up at the moonlit sky with wide open eyes that did not see. Two down, two to go, and maybe Trump Foster was ready for battle. But the toughest of them all would be Morgan Mills.

Holt wet his dry lips as he scanned the street. It was quiet; it was too damned quiet. Morg Mills must be stalking Holt, for he knew he'd never have another chance if Holt was still free with a hot rifle in his hands. This was the final hand. But where the hell was Trump Foster?

Minutes ticked past. Holt padded softly

behind a shed and peered around the corner in time to see a swift movement close by the biggest building across the street. Someone dressed all in gray. That would be Morgan Mills.

Quiet again. Holt looked toward the mine structures and caught sight of a beard bobbing up and down in there. So the old billy goat was alive anyway and so were Susan and Tim. The wind fluttered her loose skirt, and he knew she was lying flat beside her brother behind some timber balks. But Trump Foster was closer to them than he was to Holt and if he came to life . . .

Holt eased behind one building after another until he was beyond the building in which Morgan Mills was hiding and closer to the mine. He eyed each building in turn on the far side of the street, then took a chance and walked toward the mine. He was halfway across the street when something made him turn quickly. Trump Foster was standing near the body of Pete Shalen with Pete's six-shooter in his hand. He fired at Holt and Holt felt the whip of lead through the slack of his shirt. He fired but Trump, swift for one of his size, had darted for cover.

Holt heard a noise behind him. He whirled, rifle at hip level, in time to see Morg Mills standing in a doorway. Mills fired once and the slug struck savagely. The forty-four had ripped into Holt's left shoulder, high up, but enough to drive him reeling back. Pain and faintness flooded through him and he knew he couldn't stay long on his feet.

Mills snapped another shot and it skinned along Holt's left forearm like a red-hot iron. Still Holt kept his feet peering dazedly at Mills while blood dripped from his left hand and stained the earth at his feet. Once more Mills fired, and this time he missed. His Colt clicked dryly and he vanished from sight to reload.

Holt steadied his rifle, held it at about the waist level of a man who'd be standing inside that building and with the last of his strength fired, levered and fired again and again until the Winchester clicked dryly. Splinters flew from the thin wood. There was a sharp cry just once and then a man was framed in the doorway. A man in gray, but the waist of shirt and vest was black with blood. He held his hands to his belly and stepped out onto the porch, one step at a time, then stepped down into the street. He walked slowly through the rifting smoke and his eyes looked as though they were peering from a smoky window of hell itself. Step by step until he was ten feet from Holt Deaver. Then he stopped.

"You killed Mike," said Morgan Mills slowly and distinctly. "You can't kill me too, Deaver."

Holt was bracing himself on the empty rifle and the street seemed to reel and waver. Blood was soaking through his clothing and running warmly down his body.

"You can't kill me too, Deaver," repeated Morgan Mills. Then he pitched forward on his face, stiffened spasmodically and lay still forever.

"Holt!" cried Susan.

He turned slowly and saw Trump Foster walking slowly toward him with cocked Colt in a paw of a hand. "How do you want it, Deaver?" taunted Trump. "Head or belly?"

Holt dropped the rifle and clawed for his Colt, but he knew he'd never make it.

"Head or belly, Deaver?"

The big man was hardly moving now and there was a wide grin on his loose face. "Thanks," he said. "That was a nice job you done. You got rid of all the shareholders. Thanks again, Deaver." He raised the Colt.

But something moved swiftly across the moonlit street. A skinny old man with a fluttering beard and a large rusted piece of machinery which he bore like a medieval mace. It didn't seem possible Cass Riker could lift it, much less run with it.

Trump grinned again. "Ready?" he said.

"Sure as hell am, Foster!" screamed Cass Riker.

As Trump whirled in surprise the gear came down with all the power Cass had in his body, and the mass of metal flattened the big man like a poleaxe.

That was the last, or almost the last thing Holt Deaver remembered as he fell slowly. The last thing was the cry of a woman. "You can't die, Holt! You just can't die! I won't let you!"

13

HOLT DEAVER opened his eyes and knew at once where he was. It was the pleasant room where he had recuperated once before, in the Morris ranch house. It was bright daylight. He moved a little, then winced in pain as his shoulder and arm objected to the movement. He looked curiously down at them. They were swathed in neat clean bandages.

A shadow caught the corner of his left eye and he turned a little to see Susan Morris coming toward him.

"He's awake!" she called over her shoulder. She placed a deliciously cool hand on his forehead. "And no fever!" She kissed him gently.

He smiled. "That'll bring the fever right back," he said.

"Are you strong enough to talk?" she asked.

"With you? Always!"

She shook her head. "There is a gentleman here to see you."

Holt had a peculiar feeling as though she was holding back something. "All right," he said.

"You may come in, Marshal," she said.

Oh Christ, thought Holt. Where in hell were his pants and horse? But he knew he was trapped at last.

Burl Stuart came to the bedside and looked down at Holt. "How are you, Deaver?" he asked.

"Not lively enough to travel to Yuma yet."

"No. But what makes you think you're going there?"

Holt eyed him. "You didn't come here to ask about my health."

"Happens I did . . . today, anyway."

Tim Morris came into the room and stood beside his sister, grinning at Holt.

Burl Stuart hooked a thumb beneath his belt. "You've been cleared of that paymaster robbery and killing, Deaver."

"How so?"

"Trump Foster lived long enough to ask us to take his boots off and tell his story. Said he didn't want to die with it on his conscience."

Holt closed his eyes. "Thank God," he said. "What about the other mess?"

"Wells-Fargo has their money back if that's what you mean."

Holt nodded. "How much was it anyway?"

"Eighty thousand, or close to it anyway."

"There was eighty thousand when I last remember," said Holt. He grinned weakly. "I ought to know. I counted it three times."

"Eighty thousand when *you* counted it. Seventy-five thousand when *we* counted it."

Holt opened his eyes. "I haven't got it, Stuart, I'm clean."

"Well, we have an idea who got it."

"Not dead men."

"No. A real live one. Ex-outlaw by the name of Cass Riker."

Holt moved so quickly that he felt a

rush of pain through his left side. "Where is he?"

Stuart shrugged. "Where are the snows of yesteryear? He skinned out after he helped Susan and Tim here get you back to the ranch. I don't know how you're alive, Deaver."

Holt smiled at the two Morrises.

Stuart held out an envelope. "This is for you."

Holt took it and opened it. A thousand dollars was in it. "What's this for?"

"The government had offered it for the men who robbed the paymaster and did those killings. Dead or alive, Deaver."

Holt fingered the bills. He hated blood money.

"Don't feel badly. You did the country a service."

"I suppose so." Holt looked up at the marshal. "How about that Chloride business?"

Stuart looked surprised. "*What* Chloride business?" He winked broadly.

"*Gracias!*"

"It is nothing." Stuart gripped Holt's

hand. "I'm leaving now, Deaver. You'll be all right before too long. Who wouldn't be in these pleasant surroundings?" He bent close to Holt's ear and whispered something and Holt's face nearly split with a wide grin.

After Stuart was gone Susan came to sit by Holt's bedside. "What was that last thing he told you, Holt?" she asked curiously.

He shook his head. "I'd rather not tell you right now. I will later. It will be improved by the keeping."

She kissed him gently. "What are your plans, Holt?"

He looked up at her. "I'd like to know yours first."

She held his gaunt face in her lovely hands. "I think we can talk about them together, Holt, because I think we will be discussing our plans for many years to come."

It was Holt Deaver, ex-lone rider, who did the kissing that time.

The winter had passed, although snow

still lay in the passes and high on the mountain sides. Holt Deaver, rancher, rode south along the East Fork of the Bandera looking for strays. He breathed deeply of the windy, cold air. This was his home now. He shrugged his sheepskin collar higher about his neck and felt for the makings. He rolled a smoke and lighted it, eyeing with pleasure the swift and clear racing of the East Fork. It was a good land and in time it would open up so Susan could have the company of other ranch women. Tim had gone to school and wouldn't be back until summer.

He splashed through the stream and rode south along a rock face, not far from the dangerous trail he had last taken to hunt for Cass Riker. He shook his head as he thought of the old coot who had dropped out of sight as though spirited to another planet.

Although Holt was no longer a scout and the last of the rim-rock Tontos had been herded onto reservations, there was still that keen intuition in him, that feeling for the warnings that came to men with hand-honed senses. That was what now made him suddenly scan the broken ledge of rock, thickly stippled with scrub trees, not fifty yards to his left.

Something fluttered amongst the trees, and it wasn't moss. This mass of material had a pair of gimlet-sharp eyes peering just above it.

"Hello, Old Whiskers," said Holt with a grin.

Cass Riker stood up and looked quickly up and down the canyon. "We alone?" he demanded.

"Yes. Where you been, you old billy goat?"

"Running like hell. Bub, as much as I hate to admit it, I ain't got the snap and spring like I had when I took care of all them sidewinders that night up at the mine."

"*All* of them?"

"Well, what the hell, I got a *little* help from you."

"*Gracias*," said Holt dryly.

"Can I come stay at the place for awhile?"

"Sure. Lose all your money?"

Cass looked furtive. "Well, not *all* of it."

"Climb up behind, then. The law won't be around."

Cass clambered up behind Holt like a whiskered, little tin monkey. "How come?" Cass demanded suspiciously.

Holt grinned as he remembered what he had told Susan not so long ago. "They ain't interested in you, old-timer."

"I got away with five thousand bucks!"

Holt turned. "Sure, you damned old fool, but Wells-Fargo had offered that for reward, and they agreed you had it coming! They figured you served fifteen years for that robbery and were useful in getting the money back to them. So you were in the clear all the time!"

"You big dumb-block! How come you never told me?"

Holt laughed so hard his shoulder pained him. "Because you never let us know where you were, you old billy goat!"

Cass swore under his breath. "You

mean I been running all over Arizona and Sonora thinking they wanted me while I was a free man all the time?"

"You got it right, old timer. Now Missus Deaver will be right glad to see you."

"Missus Deaver?"

"Missus *Susan* Deaver!"

"I always thought that girl had more brains than that!"

Holt shook his head. "She didn't." He paused, then passed the makings back to the old man. "Welcome home, Old Whiskers."

They rode slowly home beside the East Fork of the Bandera, and both of them felt as though a piece that had been lost from each of them had at last been found.

FARGO: MASSACRE RIVER
by John Benteen

Fargo spurred his horse to the edge of the road. The ambushers up ahead had now blocked the road. Fargo's convoy was a jumble, a perfect target for the insurgents' weapons!

SUNDANCE:
DEATH IN THE LAVA
by John Benteen

The land echoed with the thundering hoofs of Modoc ponies. In minutes they swooped down and captured the wagon train and its cargo of gold. But now the halfbreed they called Sundance was going after it, and he swore nothing would stand in his way.

GUNS OF FURY
by Ernest Haycox

Dane Starr, alias Dan Smith, wanted to close the door on his past and hang up his guns, but people wouldn't let him. Good men wanted him to settle their scores for them. Bad men thought they were faster and itched to prove it. Starr had to keep killing just to stay alive.

FARGO: PANAMA GOLD
by John Benteen

Cleve Buckner was recruiting an army of killers, gunmen and deserters from all over Central America. With foreign money behind him, Buckner was going to destroy the Panama Canal before it could be completed. Fargo's job was to stop Buckner—and to eliminate him once and for all!

FARGO: THE SHARPSHOOTERS
by John Benteen

The Canfield clan, thirty strong, were raising hell in Texas. One of them had shot a Texas Ranger, and the Rangers had to bring in the killer. Fargo was tough enough to hold his own against the whole clan.

SUNDANCE: OVERKILL
by John Benteen

Sundance's reputation as a fighting man had spread. There was no job too tough for the halfbreed to handle. So when a wealthy banker's daughter was kidnapped by the Cheyenne, he offered Sundance $10,000 to rescue the girl.

HELL RIDERS
by Steve Mensing

Wade Walker's kid brother, Duane, was locked up in the Silver City jail facing a rope at dawn. Wade was a ruthless outlaw, but he was smart, and he had vowed to have his brother out of jail before morning!

DESERT OF THE DAMNED
by Nelson Nye

The law was after him for the murder of a marshal—a murder he didn't commit. Breen was after him for revenge—and Breen wouldn't stop at anything . . . blackmail, a frameup . . . or murder.

DAY OF THE COMANCHEROS
by Steven C. Lawrence

Their very name struck terror into men's hearts—the Comancheros, a savage army of cutthroats who swept across Texas, leaving behind a bloodstained trail of robbery and murder.

SUNDANCE: SILENT ENEMY
by John Benteen

Both the Indians and the U.S. Cavalry were being victimized. A lone crazed Cheyenne was on a personal war path against both sides. They needed to pit one man against one crazed Indian. That man was Sundance.

LASSITER
by Jack Slade

Lassiter wasn't the kind of man to listen to reason. Cross him once and he'd hold a grudge for years to come—if he let you live that long. But he was no crueler than the men he had killed, and he had never killed a man who didn't need killing.

LAST STAGE TO GOMORRAH
by Barry Cord

Jeff Carter, tough ex-riverboat gambler, now had himself a horse ranch that kept him free from gunfights and card games. Until Sturvesant of Wells Fargo showed up. Jeff owed him a favour and Sturvesant wanted it paid up. All he had to do was to go to Gomorrah and recover a quarter of a million dollars stolen from a stagecoach!

McALLISTER ON THE COMANCHE CROSSING
by Matt Chisholm

The Comanche, deadly warriors and the finest horsemen in the world, reckon McAllister owes them a life—and the trail is soaked with the blood of the men who had tried to outrun them before.

QUICK-TRIGGER COUNTRY
by Clem Colt

Turkey Red hooked up with Curly Bill Graham's outlaw crew and soon made a name for himself. But wholesale murder was out of Turk's line, so when range war flared he bucked the whole border gang alone . . .

PISTOL LAW
by Paul Evan Lehman

Lance Jones came back to Mustang for just one thing—Revenge! Revenge on the people who had him thrown in jail; on the crooked marshal; on the human vulture who had already taken over the town. Now it was Lance's turn . . .